I0638424

# BLACK OHIO SKIES

A Collection of Short Stories by

Sarah Wolf

In memory of Betty Zboray

and

In dedication to my years at Kent State University (1998-2002)

with special thanks to Bob King

Copyright 2012 by Sarah Wolf

*Forward by the Author*

    This collection of stories originated during my undergraduate tenure at Kent State University. One day, I was listening to the Counting Crows song "Goodnight, Elisabeth" and really paying close attention to the lyrics. I began wondering if this Elisabeth character was still alive or if she'd passed away. I had other friends read the lyrics or listen to the song to get their impressions and everyone had different ideas. I spent some time considering other Counting Crows song lyrics after that and from this came the idea that I could write a collection of stories based loosely on Adam Durtiz' words – a true homage to one of my favorite lyricists. *Black Ohio Skies* contains fourteen stories, each inspired by a Counting Crows song. A lyric from each song is credited at the first page of every narrative.

> *"Spread your wings and rise*
> *Rise into the black Ohio skies"*

*And every time she sneezes I believe
it's love, and oh lord, I'm not ready
for this sort of thing...*
        *"Anna Begins"*

She sat wrapped in a flannel blanket that smelled like him and drew her arms tightly around her body. Her eyes were tired but thoughtful, gathering every aspect of the quiet room into a tiny envelope to be stored forever in her memory. The late afternoon sun squinted through the loose folds of the blinds, making the walls striped with dulled yellow light. His poster of Ben Folds 5 was half-lost in the glare. She wished for a moment that she was not so comfortable in this place, in his bed, dressed in his shirt, with his sweat still fresh on her skin. She knew every inch of the room, every model airplane strung from the ceiling, every CD -- organized this week by alphabetical order according to color of the side label -- every dirty sock under the bed. Her eyes rested for a moment on a picture sitting beside the bed of the three of them: Ben, Sam, and her, three sweat-soaked faces pressed together and beaming under the pretense of summer. The photo was recent, and she frowned at the brevity of the single moment pinned down and slipped into a frame. The shadows on the wall shifted quietly as she remained unthawed.

She didn't know how long she had been sitting there, waiting for him. He had been shaking as he told her to wait, shaking as he'd slunk out of the room. She felt his fear in every painfully drawn breath. Sitting there, wrapped in his blanket that smelled like him, she remembered the first day they'd met, nearly seven years before, and wondered helplessly why things ever had to change.

Just as today, Anna had been over at his house because of his older brother Ben. Anna and Ben were in the same class in school, and on that distant fall day they had to build a volcano for science class. Baking soda and vinegar. For Anna, working with Ben added a certain amount of strain to the project because her eleven-year-old mind was drawn to this brown-haired, green-eyed boy with dimples in both cheeks. By the end of the afternoon, though, it was Ben's wild, charismatic brother who had put Anna at ease. Three years younger than them, Sam was red-haired and freckled. That afternoon, building the volcano, Sam had taken Anna's serious hand and dragged her out to the backyard to show her how to fry ants with a magnifying glass. *More fun than any science project a dumb old teacher could assign*, he'd said, an impish grin cascading from his face to her own.

Now, years later, wrapped in his blanket, she shivered at the memory, as dim as the shadows on the wall, and wished he hadn't broken that magnifying glass against the pavement last summer. Ben had laughed at the empty round frame that once held the lens, laughed because their parents had always told them to be careful not to break things, and he knew that Sam had smashed it on purpose. Ben had laughed and told Sam to respect his property and value the things that belonged to him, to think about the consequences of his actions. Sam had grinned. Anna had picked up the glass fragments from the driveway.

She turned her head away from the walls and stared down at the ground. He had left his sneakers by the bed. They were his favorite pair, his "never-leave-home- without-'ems," and she wondered what he had on his feet now. Maybe he had slipped on her sandals the way she'd slipped on his shirt. Maybe he was trying to walk around in her feet for awhile. Maybe he needed to put his soles against her soles and see what he had been unable to see. That was why she'd put on his shirt, to feel something that had been so close to his skin against her own, to become part of him. It was a Ridgewood High School baseball shirt. He was the starting right fielder, number four hitter. The only thing that meant more to him in life than baseball was her, so she put the shirt on to feel him better. To understand. To help.

She heard the front door click open quietly and her heart stopped beating as she drew the blanket even more tightly around her body. She heard his feet rocking slowly on the linoleum downstairs and then the sound of his bare feet hitting the carpeting on his way up the steps. His bedroom was three steps to the left of the staircase; he was close. She heard the sound of his brain ticking just outside. His fingers wrapped around the edge of the door, hesitating before pushing it open. He stood there, his eyes red, nearly as red as his hair, and stared at her. He didn't move towards her, and she drew the blanket even closer to her body. He rocked slightly in the frame, pressing his hands against the doorjamb, looking from her face to the floor. When his gaze finally rested on his shoes by the bed, he spoke.

"You're still leaving." His face was serious and drawn.

She smiled softly. "Yes."

"Tomorrow, then."

"Yes."

He nodded as he moved into the room. He kicked the shoes by his bed and planted his hands on either side of her cocoon. His eyes were innocently tarnished, bloodshot and raw. She wanted to tear her gaze away, but she couldn't. His nose was practically touching hers. "Tomorrow," he said, his lips nearly brushing her own.

She loosed the blanket from her shoulders and drew him onto the bed beside her. "Yes."

"I want to keep you here with me, Anna." He had to wipe his nose. "Tell me why I'm not enough of a reason."

She smiled at him, brushing his hair away from his eyes. "We can't be kids forever, Sam. Things change."

"We're always changing." He inched away from her. "Just sitting here in my room, we've changed."

Her eyes gently searched his and she flinched at the pain she saw. "Weren't you the first one to congratulate me on getting into Stanford? Didn't you say to me, 'Anna, we're gonna package you up and send you off to California and we're gonna tell people we knew you when.' You were so happy for me because you knew it's what I've always wanted. And now you're angry?"

He stared at her. "Things between us have most recently changed."

She looked away from him.

The silence fluttered on butterfly wings as Sam reached over and placed a quiet hand on her cheek. He smiled sadly. "My brother was never dead before."

Anna leaned towards him. She gently placed her arms around his neck and rocked slowly. "I know. I miss him, too."

Sam allowed her to meld with him. "Yeah."

"Is that what this was about today?" She whispered the words cautiously into his ear.

His body slumped. "Is that really what you think?"

She turned him to face her. "What should I think?"

Sam had called her that dazzling August morning because he said he missed Ben, said he needed to talk about him. Anna had left her packing and gone to him immediately. Ben had been dead for only two weeks. He had been out running in the morning alone; Sam normally ran with him, but he had opted for more sleep that day. It was odd, really, because Sam was Ben's cheerleader, his sociable drill sergeant. Normally, he had his running shoes on and his peppy chatter going before they even hit the road. Not that morning, though. Ben had gotten up on his own; gotten peppy on his own. He was running up a hill and was struck by a car coming over the other side. The driver had hit-and-run. After Ben lay bleeding quietly in a stranger's driveway, someone called too late for help. Ben died in the ambulance.

Sam stopped running.

"I called you because... You're here because I love you, Anna." He was mumbling. It came out like, "I callu cuz... Yurear cuz I lubu, 'Na."

She brushed her hand across his face and back through his hair. "This isn't love, Sam."

His eyes, startled and hurt, looked through her. "It is for me. Every time you so much as sneeze, I want you more. You're here right now because I love you."

She withdrew her hand from his body and tucked it tightly against her own. "I'm here right now because of Ben, Sam. I'm here because you miss him and you needed someone to be here with you. And you know that for you, I'd do anything..."

"Except stay."

"Except stay."

Sam nodded slowly and got up from the bed. He walked across the room and sat down at his computer. His bright red swivel chair had lost a screw from the bottom and wobbled slightly when he sat on it; she knew he liked it that way. His tear-away running pants were unbuttoned half way up his thigh. He was thoughtfully scratching the bare skin on his legs with his big toe, his face strangely serene.

Anna stood up and moved over near him and sat on the floor by his feet.

He looked at her. "That's my shirt," he said, almost amused.

"I didn't think you'd mind."

"Where is your shirt?"

She pointed to the corner underneath the Ben Folds 5 poster; her clothes lay in a neat pile there. She folded her arms across her knees. "You say it's love, but... I know. There are consequences to love," she said. "I mean, real love isn't something we can figure out sitting here in your room the day before I leave for school."

He stared at her, an ironic smile tilting his features. "I'm not going to worry about it. You don't want to talk about it? Then it isn't love, I get it."

She watched his toe scrape against his leg again and again. "It's just that love is all or nothing, Sam..."

"So that must make us nothing, right, Anna?" His voice cut through the air.

*For one time only, Ben had made an exception and taken Anna to their senior prom. They'd been friends, just friends, for so long that Ben's easy smile and shining eyes greeted Anna as the perpetual eleven-year-old girl who helped his brother fry ants on the pavement. But Anna longed for more, wanted more from him and had asked him to make the exception, step out of their friend mold, for one night and take her to the prom. She had leaned across the aisle in Spanish class and whispered, "I'm sure there's something in a shade of gray in the friendship dictionary." She'd smiled. "We can always change our names for one night, if we want--be something in between." Will you take me to the prom, she'd asked, and Ben had closed his eyes and smiled and said yes. Of course he would be her date, her "something in between." Anna had closed her eyes, too, and exhaled deeply, just as she did every year blowing out the candles on her birthday cake as she made her wish. I wish for Ben to love me. And on that special prom night, he had been a gentleman and kissed her good-night. Love is all or nothing.*

Anna thought about that night, about that kiss, and felt a tremor run through her. She looked at Sam.

"What do you wish for every year when you blow out your birthday candles?"

He looked at the pile of her clothes on the floor. "I wish for today."

When she had arrived at his house that morning, he had been alone. He told her the silence was bugging him, making him remember too much. She had hugged him and told him it would be OK. She told him that Ben wanted him to remember, but he shouldn't have to remember alone, and it was good that he called her. With tears streaming down his face, he had kissed her, on the jaw line, first, and then her cheek, and then her eyes. She felt her own set of tears gather as the pain in his gasps for air seemed to fill up her pores. He cried with his head against her chest for a long time, sobbing incomprehensible words, but she understood them all.

It was her idea to go upstairs. She took him by the hand and led him up to his bedroom, both of them quiet and resigned.

She was Sam's first lover; she felt like a killer.

After his innocent breath gave way to shaking sighs, he had gotten out of the bed that he and his brother used to use as a trampoline and told her he needed to be alone. Anna remained motionless until she heard the quiet click of the door downstairs. It was only then that she'd put on his shirt and cloaked herself in his blanket. It was only then that she really could feel him.

She could feel his shame then just as she could feel it now as he scraped his toe against his leg.

"I do love you, Anna. What do I have to do to make you love me back?" He shot her a sarcastic smile. "Change my name? To Ben?"

Anna's face twisted. "Don't even think that, Sam."

"It's true though, isn't it? That's what you wished for every year--for my brother. And he's dead so you settle for me. Was I as good as you thought he would be?"

Her eyes turned down. "Sam, don't."

"I can't even sleep in a quiet room anymore because all I can do is think about Ben and you. And you. It feels like you are all that's left in the world for me and now you're going away." His voice had escalated to the point where it began to echo out into the hallway. "I wish I could be Ben, but I can't, Anna."

"No one is asking you..."

"You're wrong. You asked me. And you're right--there are consequences here, even though you say this isn't love." His voice grew quiet and strained.

"I'm sorry, Sam," she said, her head still bowed. She got up and started to lift his shirt over her head, but he was suddenly behind her, touching her arm.

"Keep it," he said. And then he turned and walked out of the room.


The next day as she prepared to leave for the airport, she thought about calling him, just as she had thought about calling him every other second the previous day and all that morning. But as her hand touched the phone and glossed over the numbers, she felt the muddled loved she harbored for both the brothers bubble up in her throat and knew she wasn't ready to deal with it. Not yet. Ten years from now, she wouldn't be ready.

As she loaded the last few things into her father's SUV, she thought she heard a voice call out from across the street.

*"In this fog, you're already starting to fade from my life, and you haven't even left."*

She turned and saw no one was there. Still, she answered, "What do you mean?" She shrugged her shoulders up towards the clear, blue sky. "It's a beautiful day."

*"Seems sunless to me."*

She titled her head upwards. "Please forgive me."

Standing in the driveway, she waited for her father to emerge from the house and wondered if it didn't seem a bit foggy after all.

Big Dipper By Day

*Hey Mrs. Potter don't go*
*Hey Mrs. Potter I don't know but*
*Hey Mrs. Potter won't you talk to me*
            *"Mrs. Potter's Lullaby"*

Andy woke up in mid-afternoon without the aid of an alarm clock and pulled a dirty white t-shirt off the floor and over his head. He slid his feet into a forlorn-looking pair of sneakers and tromped downstairs to the kitchen.

"Clean your room," he said aloud, reading the note left on the table by his father. "I wouldn't even know where to begin." He chuckled as he opened the refrigerator and pulled out the carton of orange juice. Taking a giant swig from the bottle, he swished the liquid around in his mouth. Glancing out the window, he saw his neighbor Anna Matthews and her father loading the last few items into the family SUV. His eyes momentarily shifted out of focus until he glanced back over at the note from his father. *Clean your room.* Clenching his teeth, he pushed out the door without brushing his teeth or combing his matted hair.

Once his feet hit the grass, he paused to watch Anna and her father drive off down the block. Shivering slightly, despite the warmth of the late summer air, he began walking in the opposite direction down the block. As each step hit the concrete, his pace increased until he was jogging, past the house where Ben used to live and through the parking lot of the elementary school. He resisted the urge to ride the tire swing and kept running through the field behind the school to the familiar white house in the grove of weeping willows. He tripped up the steps on the wooden patio on the back of the house and knocked on the sliding glass door until a short, white-haired lady wearing overalls and a pink shirt appeared.

"Hello, Andrew. You look out of breath this morning." The door glided open and she smiled, her wrinkled face appearing youthful in the light.

"Mrs. Potter. It's, like, two-thirty. It's not morning anymore."

"For you, Andrew, it's morning. I was about to work in my garden. Come and talk to me there."

Andy followed Mrs. Potter's fluid movements as she picked up a pair of garden shears, a pair of gloves, and a bucket and headed down off the porch. He jumped off the steps and stood awkwardly behind her as she sat down in the grass and began her daily ritual of weeding and trimming her garden.

"What brings you by today, Andrew?" she asked without looking up.

Andy hopped nervously from one foot to the other. "Ah, I dunno, Mrs. Potter. I just haven't been by in awhile, and I thought I should come and say hi."

"Uh huh," she murmured.

Still hopping, Andy furrowed his lips. "Anna left for school today."

Mrs. Potter turned her head slightly to the side. "Oh? Anna Matthews, I presume?"

Andy nodded. "She's going to some Ivy League school or something. That's what Ben said."

"She was always a smart girl," Mrs. Potter said, resuming her work.

"She's dumb," Andy grumbled.

Mrs. Potter chuckled. "Now, Andrew..."

He kicked the grass in front of him. "I'm just jealous because I know that when I graduate next year, I'll have to stay home. I think that bites, if I can be blunt."

Mrs. Potter's hands busily plucked weeds from between her flowers. "You can be."

"I just wish I could afford to go to school. That's all," he said with a shrug.

"Well, keep saving your pennies, dear. Isn't your father supposed to be getting a promotion? Maybe he'd help you."

"Nah, he got passed over for the promotion this time. He said he didn't want to be district manager of a crummy grocery store, anyway. He said he might quit working there and open a bait and tackle shop. I don't want to make him spend that kind of money on me, anyway. I mean, I'll apply for scholarships and stuff, but I don't think we're poor enough to get much. I thought maybe my mom would help, but her new husband is the one with the cash and he won't give me a dime. So I've decided just to be a bum for the rest of my life." He lay down in the grass behind Mrs. Potter with his hands tucked behind his head.

"Andrew, you're a bum now, and it makes you miserable," she said, pulling out a few tiny weeds by the roots.

"Ouch, Mrs. Potter," he said, shaking his head.

"Really, though. Have you thought about what would make you happy?"

Andy tilted his head. "Sure, but there are about a million things to consider. And a million things you can't help. I mean, look at what happened to Ben this summer. I saw him and Sammy the day before the accident and they were thinking about buying this ugly-looking cat for their mom from that pet shop where Lisa works, since they're not allowed to have a dog, just so they could laugh at the look on her face while she tried to thank them. I mean, they were so happy. And what happened the next damn day?"

"What happened to Benjamin was a terrible thing, Andrew," Mrs. Potter said, picking up her shears. "But he'd be pretty angry at you if he knew that you were using his tragedy as an excuse to discount happiness."

Andy swallowed. "Ben was my best friend."

Her shoulders sank as she sighed. "I know, dear. And I know his funeral was hard for you, but I also believe that you will be just fine as time goes by."

"It'll be weird not to see him around, that's all," Andy said. "I mean, I know he was leaving for Notre Dame and all, but that was different. He was still coming back, then."

"It's hard to lose a friend, especially one so close," Mrs. Potter said.

"Imagine how hard it is for Sam," Andy said. "I don't have a brother, but I'd imagine that's harder than losing a friend."

Mrs. Potter clucked her tongue. "Different. Not harder."

"I don't want to talk about him anymore right now." Andy closed his eyes.

Mrs. Potter paused to look at him. "All right."

He propped himself up on his elbows. "You know, sometimes I feel like life is this big social gathering and when it's my turn to play the host, I never get to see the guest list and no one there knows me, anyway. I just plow through the crowd with a tray of teeny weenies and an empty bottle of champagne with a name tag that says, 'Hi, I'm

Me.' And everyone is having a good time at the party except for me because I'm too busy thinking."

Mrs. Potter continued her work. "Just make sure you remember to think about the happy times, too."

"Trust me, if I could escape from the sad stuff, I would. But I think you can only avoid it for so long before it catches up with your new location in the time-space continuum. That's what Dr. Spock would say, at least."

She laughed. "Leave it to science fiction!"

He cleared his throat. "Sammy never really liked me, not the whole time we were growing up. But maybe now I should see if I can be his friend. He probably needs one, especially since Anna's leaving."

"They were close," Mrs. Potter agreed.

"Yeah, and Ben wouldn't have left for school for another two weeks, so Sam would have had time to get used to her being gone. And Ben said he was going to make me Sam's pseudo-big-brother for when he was gone and we were supposed to get the ball rolling on that after Anna left. Not that Sam can't take care of himself." Andy paused. "Not that I can really be of any use to him, brother-wise. But I could have listened to him, looked out for him, and called Ben at Notre Dame and got Sam the advice he needed. If he needed it."

Mrs. Potter probably smiled. "I'm sure you would have been a great help for them."

Andy nodded rapidly. "Yeah. Yeah, but now, I don't know. I really don't have any good advising skills. I'm more or less terrible at it. Once, I told Curt to shave his eyebrows because they were so bushy and I thought it might help him get this girl Sandra to go out with him."

Mrs. Potter stopped what she was doing and looked at him. "You got Curtis to shave his eyebrows?"

Andy grinned. "Well, no. He's way too smart for that, it turns out. But the point is I told him he should. And that was bad advice -- I know that now. Because I tried to shave my eyebrows, that night, and my dad wouldn't buy my school pictures that year because I looked like such a goof."

Mrs. Potter went back to her work. "I remember that now."

"Oh, it's Andy-legend, for sure."

"I like when you did the fourth grade constellation project, but you renamed them all after your favorite food."

"Oh, man, you remember that? Pretty vintage stuff, Mrs. Potter," Andy said.

"Indeed."

He opened his eyes and stared at the pulsating blue sky above him. "I think I see the Big Dipper," he said.

Mrs. Potter glanced upwards. "Don't you mean Chicken Finger Basket?" she asked warily.

"Ha ha. No, I've realized the error of my ways. Really, though," he said, pointing up. "There's the handle. Wait, damn it. A cloud just covered it. But it's there." He sat up. "Mrs. Potter, it's there. Why should it need to be nighttime for us to see it? Why should we have to be out in a desert, away from the lights of the city to see it? Why should we let some stupid cloud get in the way?"

"Well, Andrew, of course it's always there."

"Do you think that you can see people's souls then, by looking at them?"

"Pardon, dear?" she said, flicking a bee away from her ear.

"Do you think you can see a person's soul just by looking at him? I mean, if you know the Big Dipper is there, you can see it even if it's day time or the lights in the city are too bright. So can you see a person's soul?" Andy sat up and crossed his legs Indian-style.

Mrs. Potter said nothing and began to hum.

"Because I think you can. I mean, I think we're all acrobats walking across tightropes with trained toy poodles balanced on our heads, and I think that we're all sufficiently trained to jump from the tightrope and catch the swinging trapeze without ever letting that poodle fall. That's what makes us human."

"I'm afraid you lost me, Andrew," she said, tossing the weeds into her bucket.

"It's simple, Mrs. Potter. You can see a person's soul by the way they walk that tight rope. Do they waver, almost fall? Do they walk confidently, slipping occasionally but always recovering? Do they act cocky, showing off, juggling the poodle? What happens when they jump to the trapeze? Do they soar like some bad-ass bird or do they look awkward and stupid in the air? And while we're on the subject, what color is the poodle? Is it black? Is it white? Is it gray? That's how you can see a person's soul." Andy plucked the grass in front of him.

Mrs. Potter faced him with her features drawn. "Yes, I suppose you're correct."

Andy paused for a moment, staring at the grass. "Do you miss Mr. Potter?"

Her nose twitched. "Every day, dear."

"See? That's what sucks about remembering stuff. There's this vindictive bastard at the memory toll booth who collects hard core because the price of a memory is steep. Hell, even the happy memories are sad because Mr. Potter is gone and you have to think about stuff alone."

Mrs. Potter turned back to her work. "You're right, Andrew."

"But you know what's nice about life?" he asked. "There's always more to do. There's always another envelope to lick, another phone call to make, another movie to see, another person to meet... So even when bad things happen or we feel our souls start to slip on that tight rope, we know that there is something to look forward to, even if we don't know what that something is."

"That's the most uplifting thing you've said so far," Mrs. Potter said, stretching her arms briefly above her head.

"I'm not trying to be a downer, Mrs. Potter... I'm just saying what I'm thinking..."

"No wonder it hurts you so much to think, Andrew..."

"I'm just glad that you let me talk to you."

"Of course, Andrew."

"Because you're probably the best listener in the world," he continued. "If you hadn't been around my whole life, I probably would be in the loony bin by now. You're, like, my hero. In fact, if I thought you'd go for a teenager, I'd woo you, seriously."

Mrs. Potter laughed. "Oh, really?"

He smiled as he rubbed a blade of grass between his fingers. "Sure, why not? It's not like I have a girlfriend anyway. Not that you'd ever be a consolation prize..."

"No offense taken, Andrew."

"I'm just dateless."

"Maybe you're a late bloomer, dear," Mrs. Potter said, throwing another handful of weeds into the bucket.

"Or maybe I'm already a little wilty." He flicked the blade of grass out of the palm of his hand. "Do you think elephants really never forget?"

"Elephants?"

"Yeah. You know how they always say that elephants never forget? You think that's true?"

"I'm not really sure what an elephant has to remember, Andrew," Mrs. Potter said seriously.

"Yeah, I thought about that. I mean, it doesn't have to remember stuff like when the Declaration of Independence was signed or how to do trigonometry, it only has to remember where to find good food and who's in charge of the herd. But the captured ones in the zoo have to remember what it was like to be free as they're being handed their food by the handler who's in charge. Do you think the captive ones try to forget to remember?" Andy tipped his head towards the school playground as a couple of children jumped on the tire swing.

Mrs. Potter appeared thoughtful. "I probably would, if I were an elephant used to freedom."

"I guess not even the animals have it easy, huh. I mean, if it's true that elephants never forget, then the captive ones have to be about ten times more depressed than even me! Because I can't imagine someone putting me in a zoo." His head swiveled towards Mrs. Potter's back.

Mrs. Potter smiled. "That would be quite awful."

Andy assumed a squatting position and attempted to do a headstand. When he flopped to the ground with an awkward somersault, he cleared his throat and asked, "Did you go to the Fest this summer, Mrs. Potter?"

"No, dear," she said without looking at him.

"I went with some friends from school. Ben, too. And I remember a few of the guys would not get off of that tilt-a-whirl ride. You ever been on it?"

"No, dear."

"It's this crazy-ass ride that spins you around until you puke up your corn dog. A couple of the guys just rode that damn thing about ten times in a row. They said it was better than smoking dope, the high they got off the spinning around." He paused. "I smoked pot once, and I couldn't figure out how they even compared. But I'm not as experienced in that sort of thing as those guys. I rode the ferris wheel, though, with this tenth-grade chick named Tammy. I thought about putting the moves on her, but she has braces and all I could do was stare at her damn teeth. I never wore braces because my father thinks crooked teeth are a good reminder that life doesn't always go straight up and down. And I just stared at her teeth the whole time and ran my tongue over my own crooked teeth and wished my father had gotten me braces. I actually wanted to ask her all these questions about her braces, like if they made eating hard or if they cut up the inside of her lip and stuff. But I didn't ask her any of that. I just bullshitted about school and stuff. She's only in tenth grade, so she was impressed by anything I had to say."

"I never had braces, either," Mrs. Potter said.

"Then you know what I'm talking about," Andy said, bobbing his head up and down. "You know what I'm talking about. Hey, did I ever tell you I dream in shades of blue?"

"I don't think you ever have, Andrew."

"Well, truth be told, I don't dream in shades of blue. But it would be cool if I did. Like Picasso's blue period. We learned about it in my Spanish class last year. Weird thing to study in Spanish, eh, Mrs. Potter?"

"Wasn't Picasso Spanish, dear?" Mrs. Potter asked absentmindedly.

Andy pursed his lips. "Well, yeah. But it's still a weird thing to learn in a class that is supposed to be about conjugating verbs and vocabulary words. But me and Ben used to sit in that class and talk about how cool it would be to have our own blue period. I mean, blue's a somber color, a reflective color. That's what Ben and I thought. And I bet if I dreamt in blue, I'd remember my dreams better. Maybe I'd even remember Ben better. It's easier to remember things with consistency, like a color consistency, don't you think?"

"Uh huh."

"Mrs. Potter, do you think I have a warped perception of life? You can be honest." Andy lay down and propped his hands under his head once more.

She paused and glanced at him. "I think you have a unique perception, Andrew."

"Which is a nice way of saying I'm warped. That's OK. That's sort of what I thought. I think I'm just too sensitive."

Mrs. Potter resumed her work. "You're a good boy, Andrew."

"I remember a New Year's Party my mom and her new husband had a few years back that my mom made me come over for and her new husband was the life of that party all right. He was throwing 'em back like the world was ending at midnight. I was about the only kid there, so I just sat on this uncomfortable couch of my mother's, the only thing she took when she left besides a picture of me, and watched him drink and drink. He's a lawyer or a stockbroker or something so all his rich lawyer-stockbroker friends were there and they were all wearing these embarrassing button-down shirts like it was an office meeting instead of a party. And around two in the morning, long after he should have realized that the world was not ending and he'd gotten sloppy-drunk enough, he took the shot glass he'd been using to pound bourbon and just smashed it against the floor. He has these hard, marble floors in most of the house, so the glass really shattered. I thought maybe that meant the party was over and I got up to go upstairs to the guest room and as I headed up the stairs, I saw my mother pour him another drink. Now, Mrs. Potter, what for?" he asked.

"I'm afraid excessive drinking has never been something I understood, Andrew," she said, pulling another straggling weed out of the ground.

"Well, I went right up to bed and slammed my door and put my pillow over my head and went to sleep. The next morning, I got up before them and left my mom a note and walked to the bus station and came home. It was a terrible night, but it felt so good to walk out that door. I haven't gone back there since and I hardly ever talk to my mom. That's hard, not talking to your own mother. When Ben got hit by that car, I almost called her because I thought about how dumb it was that I never even talked to her while she's out there, alive. But I couldn't dial the number. I made my dad dial and then all I could say was, 'Hi. My friend Ben died. How are you?' I felt like an ass."

"But I bet you felt better after you talked to her."

Andy nodded. "Yeah."

He sat quietly for a long time. The only sounds were the light brushes of Mrs. Potter's hands against the flowers, against the bucket. He stared up at the clouds and tried to see pictures in the sky, but he found he could see better when he closed his eyes. Finally, he opened them.

"Say, Mrs. Potter, thanks for talking to me. I'll come back and talk to you again sometime soon, OK?" He climbed slowly to his feet and dusted the grass off of him.

"Of course, Andrew. You're always welcome here. Say hello to your father for me." Mrs. Potter said.

"I will, Mrs. Potter," he said. "Good-bye."

"Good-bye, dear."

Andy hurried back across the field, through the schoolyard, and past Ben's house. When he reached his own front yard, he saw his father's car parked in the driveway and his father smoking a cigarette on the front stoop.

"Andy, there you are," he said with a grin. "Did you go out for a jog?"

"Yeah, Dad. What are you doing home early?"

"Checking to see if you'd cleaned your room yet."

Andy smiled sheepishly. "Not yet, sir."

"Well, get cracking."

"Sure, Dad," Andy said, sitting on the step next to his father.

"Listen, kiddo, I thought maybe you and I could go camping this weekend. One last bachelor's day out before school starts. Sound good?"

"As long as we go somewhere where I can see the Big Dipper..."

His father shook his head. "You can see it now, son. Just look up in the sky -- it's there."

Andy smiled to himself as his eyes wandered across the street to Anna's house. "Do you mind if I go out for a drive? I promise I'll clean my room later."

"Sure, son," his father said, tossing him the keys.

"Thanks, Dad," he said, climbing into his father's old white Camry. He pulled out of the driveway and headed off in the direction of Anna and her father. He got onto the interstate with every intention of catching up with her at the airport and wishing her luck, since Ben couldn't. Even though he knew she was probably long gone, he merged into traffic with the radio blaring the latest disastrous pop hit, and began practicing what he would say.

"Learn lots of cool stuff," he murmured.

It wasn't long before he found himself in a summer construction zone and he slowed to a crawl. He thought about Mrs. Potter's patience with him and tried to apply it to the patience he had to summon to survive the traffic. He glanced at a green road sign and swore it said "Andy's Objective, 1,000,000 mi." below "Airport, 3 mi." High above him, though, he saw the silver outline of an airplane taking off from a nearby runway and he grinned. Rolling down his window, Andy shouted towards the sky. "When you hit cruising altitude up there, Anna, say hi to Ben for me!" Shading his eyes, he almost thought he could see her flashing a thumbs-up sign from one of the windows. His head still hanging out of the car, he looked at the road sign and saw his million miles of life were still ahead of him, and he laughed.

The War

*Get right to the heart of matters*
*It's the heart that matters more.*
*"Omaha"*

Mr. Blake leaned back in his wooden rocking chair and tipped his hat over his face. The air on the porch was muggy and heavy with humidity and summer dust, but it was still cooler than his house. He could hear his wife Luceile in the kitchen chopping carrots and celery and tossing them on top of the lettuce in a large wooden bowl. She had the evening news on at full volume as she hummed Nat King Cole melodies. He breathed quietly into his hat.

"Well, it looks like this heat wave will continue at least for the next few days, Dave," the female anchor said. "But before we get to weather, let's check in with Mary and see how the drive home will be today."

"Thanks, Debra," a new voice said. "Summer construction will delay most commuters..."

"Paul, you should see the traffic!" Luceile yelled out the window. "Makes me glad we live away from the hustle and bustle of the city."

"Uh huh," Mr. Blake said into his hat.

"Look at those poor people," Luceile continued. "All they want to do is get home..."

Mr. Blake slid the hat off his face and turned to look at the TV through the window. "When I was in the war, all I wanted to do was go home," he muttered. There was an aerial shot of the interstate that displayed clogged lanes and orange barrels.

Luceile laughed. "That traffic looks enough like a war zone. Except that young man doesn't seem to mind it much," she said, waving her knife at the screen.

Mr. Blake squinted. "What are you talking about?"

She turned her head to the side. "That boy in the white car there. He has his head stuck out of his window, like a dog."

Mr. Blake shook his head. "How can you see that?"

Luceile went back to chopping the vegetables. "I can always find the silver lining, Paul."

He grunted and looked out across his yard. He wished the weatherman saw rain in the immediate future. His own grass was a dull green, limp and tired. His eyes traveled across the road.

"The grass is always greener..." he quipped.

He rocked in his chair and stared in muted amazement at the flourishing field of corn across the wide, black top road. He saw his neighbor Darren Deetz walking through the stalks with his grandson Omaha.

"The next few days will be hot and dusty for the entire viewing area," Dave the Weatherman said, "which is bad news for the farmers..."

Mr. Blake leaned forward in his chair and watched the cornstalks bend out of the way of their commanders. Darren's worn-out Indians baseball cap bobbed above the stalks while Omaha was swallowed into the forest of vibrant green giants. Mr. Blake squinted and pressed his hands flat on his knees.

"What is it, Paul?" Luceile called from the kitchen.

He didn't move. "Just looking at Deetz' field."

"In local news, World War II veteran Paul Blake, Korean War veteran Louis Freedman and Vietnam veteran Daniel Moore, each Purple Heart recipients, will be on hand tomorrow for the unveiling of the long-awaited statue honoring the community's war heroes..."

Luceile wiped her hands on her white apron and quickly turned off the TV. Coming over to the window, she leaned against the frame and followed her husband's stubborn gaze across the street.

"It is amazing, isn't it? Did you ever ask him how he managed to get such a good crop in this terrible dry spell?" she asked.

Mr. Blake shook his head. "Man never had any sense when it came to farming, Ceile. That's what makes the least amount of sense."

Luceile chuckled. "Sandrine swears it's the boy that brought all the luck."

Mr. Blake frowned. "The boy?"

"Sure. Their grandson. Omaha. You've met him."

"Of course I've met him," Mr. Blake snapped.

Luceile ignored him. "Ever since his mama was killed in that automobile crash in the spring and he came to live with his grandparents, things seem to have turned around for them -- for their farm, I mean."

Mr. Blake narrowed his eyes and leaned back in his chair. "What does the boy have to do with the war, Ceile?"

Luceile frowned. "The farm, Paul. You mean the farm."

"That's what I said."

Luceile sighed and shrugged. "Sandrine says her grandson is magical, Paul. And I have no reason to doubt the woman."

"Except that she cheats in Bingo and has a half-insane husband," Mr. Blake muttered.

Luceile laughed. "They're good people, Paul. And I'm glad to see them doing well, as the result of a magical grandson or by the grace of God, I don't care which. Now, why don't you come on inside for supper?"

Mr. Blake's eyes lingered for a moment on the swishing of the tall crops across the road and grunted before getting up and heading in to eat.

That night, he lay in bed beside Luceile with the ceiling fan whispering cooler breezes through the suffocating heat of the room, almost as suffocating as the stealthy heat of the jungles he terrorized in World War II. Staring up at the darkness, he swore he could see the face of Darren Deetz' grandson every time he blinked his eyes. The innocent, deeply-tanned face of the eleven-year-old Omaha Oswald O'Ryan, smiling and bright-eyed, with messy brown hair and a joyful smile. Mr. Blake never thought much of him before, finding him to be nothing but a startlingly simple boy with a silly hippy name.

*"Sandrine says her grandson is magical."*

Mr. Blake stared into the darkness and grunted. Blinking his eyes, he saw flashes of Omaha as he'd seen him earlier that day, standing in the field. Only now he was looking across the street and waving, smiling, beckoning. Laughing. Mr. Blake shivered despite the heat and fell asleep with his eyes open.

The next morning, Mr. Blake woke up before his wife and swung his legs off to the side of the bed. Staring intently out the open window, he searched Deetz' home for signs of life, for signs of Omaha, but all he saw was the tentacles of sunlight streaming over the field. Putting his hand over his face, he closed his eyes and flinched as he saw Omaha staring back at him. Laughing.

"Son of a bitch," he muttered, rubbing his fingers over his face.

Luceile was still snoring, so Mr. Blake got up and made his way to the bathroom in the hallway. After splashing some water on his face and stuffing his legs into his faded overalls, he went down the creaking wooden steps towards the kitchen. He paused on the landing and stared at the plain brown floor that reminded him on a daily basis that he was back in civilization, that he was safe.

"I don't need a statue to tell me that I'm a goddamn war hero," he mumbled.

Turning his head to look out through the glass door, he saw the stalks of corn rustle, as if bending out of the way of a ranking officer, but he didn't see Darren's old hat.

"Must be the boy," Mr. Blake said.

Without picking up his own hat off the kitchen table, Mr. Blake went out the front door and across the road to Deetz' field. He followed the swaying of the stalks carefully and quietly. He could hear the sound of children laughing and talking, but his focus was on the stealth of his mission. Mr. Blake slid through the rows of corn as fluidly as he had crawled through the jungles of the Pacific. His eyes widened and a determined grimace enveloped his face as he stalked his prey: Omaha. Laughing.

The sun hung low in the sky as it yawned its way into view. He ignored the soft glare, ignored the burn of his exposed bald head, ignored the painful gasps of air being gulped by his joints. His operative was to find that boy, find that magical boy; he needed to find out what that boy had to do with Deetz' crop, what the boy had to do with him.

"My best friend died at the beach named after you, Omaha," he said.

Deetz' field banked on a tiny grouping of trees surrounding a small pond. Darren and Sandrine often invited Mr. Blake and Luceile over to picnic beside the water during the summer, although they hadn't extended such an invitation since Omaha had arrived. When Mr. Blake got to the edge of the field, he paused and bent his hands onto his knees. Taking a moment to breathe, he felt the rivulets of sweat beading up on his face and trickling down his back.

"I'm getting too old for jungle warfare," he muttered.

Straightening himself, he moved slowly towards the embankment of trees and peered into the clearing, towards the sound of the children's laughter. His eyes darted as the sound bounced off the trees until he narrowed in on a little girl with short, dark brown hair in a red sundress who was laughing and clapping at the edge of the pond. He stared at her, wondering what was so funny in the jungle, in the circle of trees around the circular pond. She was jumping, cheering, her bare feet sticking in the mud with every hop, her hands pointing to the center, the focal point, the heart of the clearing. Mr. Blake's eyes followed the invisible light flowing from the tips of her impossibly tiny hands across the water.

"Oh my God," he said, leaning his full weight against the tree.

It was Omaha. He was standing, firmly planted on the plate-glass water, in the center of the pond.

Mr. Blake watched in horrified amazement as Omaha waved intently at the little girl on the shore. "See, Edna? I told you I could still do it!" he yelled.

Mr. Blake tried to swallow his shock but his throat was too dry, and he choked on the fumes of surprise. Coughing slightly, his body doubled over as he slipped towards the ground in a crumpled heap. He lay in the dirt in abject disbelief and horror and moaned, his thick hands pressed tightly against his face. Seconds later, he pried his fingers away and stared up at a smiling face: Omaha. Laughing.

"Are you OK, Mr. Blake?" he asked, crouching beside him.

Mr. Blake sat up slowly. "Well, I, uh, yes, I'm fine, young man." He rubbed his skull and felt a small knot starting to form where he'd hit his head.

"Can you stand up, sir?" Omaha extended his hand.

Mr. Blake grunted as the boy helped pull him to his feet.

"You're really OK?" Omaha asked again.

"Yes, yes, I'm fine." Mr. Blake stood awkwardly beside the boy, staring uncertainly at his strikingly normal face.

"You want to come and play with us, then?" Omaha asked. "I mean, if you're really OK?"

"Of course I'm OK. How many times do you need to ask me if I'm OK? I'm OK!" Mr. Blake said, waving his hands in the air.

"Great," Omaha said. Laughing, he turned and bounded back through the trees to where Edna was making a small castle out of mud.

Mr. Blake eyed the children warily before joining them. Sitting on a stump near the pond's edge, he folded his arms across his chest and gestured toward the girl.

"Who's she?" he asked.

Omaha looked up, half-surprised to see Mr. Blake sitting there. "Oh, she's my sister."

"Sister?" he repeated.

"Mmm hmm," Omaha said, patting another layer of mud onto the castle. "Her name is Edna."

Mr. Blake stared at the back of the girl's head and grunted. "Who names a little boy Omaha and a little girl Edna?"

Omaha looked over at him and smiled. "My mama," he said.

Mr. Blake blinked. "Sorry, boy, I didn't mean to insult you."

Omaha stuck his fingers in the mud to carve a moat around the castle. "Oh, it's OK, Mr. Blake."

He watched the two children slather another layer of mud on top of the castle, Omaha poking holes in the side for windows, Edna smoothing out the edges. He forgot for a moment about Omaha, allowed himself to be bored, even, until his eyes traced back out to the center of the pond. He knew the pond was at least seven feet deep in the center. He himself was about six-six and had spent many a relaxing afternoon swimming with his wife and his neighbors. Mr. Blake stared across the smooth ripples of the pond and tried to detect the footprints of the boy, Omaha. Foot prints on the surface of water.

"Hey, mister," a small voice said beside him.

Turning his attention away from the invisible tracks in the water, he looked towards the voice, belonging to Edna. "Yeah," he said.

"You wanna walk on water, too?" Her large, brown eyes were playful and curious.

Mr. Blake cleared his throat. "I, uh, well, you see, um... Too?" he asked feebly.

Edna nodded. "Like Omaha," she said.

Omaha savagely poked another hole into the side of the castle. "Shut up, Edna."

Edna turned back towards her brother. "What...?"

Omaha got up and caught his sister's hand. "You can't ask him that," he said. "Not *yet*."

Mr. Blake leaned forward in earnest. "And why not?"

Omaha looked from the frightened face of Edna to the curious face of Mr. Blake. "Because it's impossible," he said.

"To ask the question or do the deed?" Mr. Blake asked.

Omaha sat quietly for a moment. "You were in World War II, like my grandpa was."

Mr. Blake straightened. "I was about seventeen when I landed at a US Marine base in Okinawa."

"What was it like?" Omaha asked.

Mr. Blake stared at the back of Edna's head as she slapped another fistful of mud onto the castle. "It was war."

Omaha folded his hands in his lap. "I mean, what was it *like*?"

Mr. Blake looked back out across the water. "It was, well... War, young man. Some days were downright dull and the highlight was swatting the mosquitoes away from your foxhole. But other days..." He stared at the soft ripples of water. "You shouldn't ask questions you don't want the answers to, son."

"What do you mean, sir?"

Mr. Blake looked back at the boy. "What I mean is... War is more real than anything else in life. And too much reality can be hard to bear. Especially for a young boy."

"Like you were?" Omaha asked.

Mr. Blake nodded briskly. "Like me."

Edna turned and faced Mr. Blake. "Did you see lots of dead people, then, in the war?"

Mr. Blake felt a slight chill sting his spine. "Well, little girl, I, uh, well, yes."

"Did you make them that way?" Her eyes gleamed.

Mr. Blake swallowed hard as his eyes jumped from innocent child's face to innocent child's face. "Well, it was a war," he said finally.

"But..." Edna began.

Omaha laughed. "I think you're making him nervous, Edna."

Edna pouted. "You started it."

"Well, I had a reason for asking," Omaha said.

"What?" Edna asked, slapping her hand on top of the mud castle.

Omaha looked at Mr. Blake. "I asked because you asked him about walking on water."

Edna nodded. "Oh."

Mr. Blake narrowed his eyes. "What does the war have to do with the, well, you know, the thing, uh, the water, I mean."

Omaha stood up and pointed towards the sky. "The clouds stay up there because someone once told them that they should stay up there. That the sky is their home."

Mr. Blake looked up and saw nothing but blue sky.

"The clouds, see, have a right to defend their home. Mama used to say that's why there were storms -- the clouds were blocking invaders."

"Like aliens?" Mr. Blake asked dubiously.

Omaha laughed. "Maybe," he said. "But Mama said it was more a way to outsmart man and keep man out of the sky. You know, airplanes and stuff."

Mr. Blake pressed his hand against his face. "Airplanes fly every day, boy."

"Right," Omaha said with a grin. Turning, he took a slow step towards the edge of the pond. Edna stopped pressing mud onto the castle and giggled as her brother stepped carefully, gingerly into the water. Mr. Blake watched in quiet panic as Omaha's feet rose above the surface and he moved across the crests of the waves. When he reached the center of the pond, he sat down and bobbed like a duck. Edna clapped and cheered. Mr. Blake's jaw dropped to the ground.

"You see, Mr. Blake, the clouds were supposed to stay in the sky and defend it. But people found a way to invade. The war you were in wasn't supposed to be your war, but the enemy found a way to invade." Omaha folded his legs like a Buddha. "People weren't supposed to walk on water, but I found a way," he said with a smile.

Mr. Blake's face flushed. "Oh, God," he said.

Omaha stood up and walked back across the pond. "My mama told me about the war you fought in a long time ago because she said it would help me understand my grandpa. She said that my grandpa lost himself in that war, your war. She said it was up to me -- me and her -- to help him." Omaha stepped off the water and walked over to Mr. Blake. "That's why I've come, you see."

Mr. Blake looked into the consuming, patient eyes of the boy and shuddered. "Listen, boy, I don't know what kind of trick you're playing here, but I don't want to be a part of it," he said.

Omaha laughed. "I can teach you to walk on water."

Mr. Blake jumped up from his seat on the stump and backed away from the children. "No," he said.

Omaha grinned. "That's what Grandpa said at first, too," he said. "But ever since he learned how, he's been happier. I can help you, too, Mr. Blake." He extended a freckled hand.

Mr. Blake stared as the child's fingers seem to reach out for him, to grow longer, to drag him into a war against himself, against nature. Omaha simply smiled with Edna leaning against him. Mr. Blake felt panic bubbling up inside of him. He felt like he was back in the jungle, was being tested by God, was tripping on a land mine.

"Leave me alone!" he said.

Omaha remained motionless, his hand stretched out before him. Edna sucked on a muddy thumb.

Mr. Blake turned and hurried out of the clearing, through the trees, and down the dusty pathway leading to Deetz' house. He ignored the pain in his aged legs as he ran, hurried towards the house, the base, away from the enemy, away from the jungle. He saw his friend's face, plastered with a serene smile, looking out of a second-story window at him. Mr. Blake ignored him and ran until the path melded into the driveway, until the driveway careened into the street.

He hurried across to his own house as a roar of thunder exploded up above. He looked up, startled to see the sky suddenly dark, consumed by the storm clouds that Dave the Weatherman had insisted were not coming anytime soon. Mr. Blake dashed up onto the porch and into the house, slamming the door behind him in time to the second rocket of thunder.

"Paul? Is that you?" Luceile called from a back room where she kept her sewing machine.

Mr. Blake leaned against the door and gulped in air faster than he was able to breathe. He closed his eyes and saw the strikingly normal face of Omaha. Laughing.

"Can you believe how quickly this storm came up? The rain will sure help our neighbors, though," Luceile said.

Mr. Blake felt his entire body begin to shake as the sweat ran through the cracks of his body, his hands pressed flat against the wall.

"I got a call from Sandrine this morning. She invited us over to lunch with Darren and their grandson this Sunday."

Mr. Blake drew a deep breath and clutched the white curtains on the door. He closed his eyes and saw a flash of Omaha with Edna leaning against him. "What about the girl?" he asked in a low voice.

"Pardon?" Luceile called.

"The little girl. Edna," he said.

The sewing machine stopped humming and Luceile came out into the hallway. Seeing her husband's panic, she hurried over to him. "Why, Paul. Are you OK?"

"Why does everyone keep asking me that?" he asked thickly. "I'm *fine*."

"Are you certain, dear? Come and sit down," she said.

He shook his head. "I'm fine, Ceile."

Luceile raised her eyebrows. "You're not, Paul. Is this about the commemoration today?"

"Forget that damn statue, woman. I asked you a question," he said, his eyes darkening.

The thunder echoed around the house.

"Yes, well, I think I understood you wrong," she said slowly, placing a cool hand on his forehead. "Paul, you're burning!"

He released the curtain and grabbed her hand. "All I want is a simple answer to my simple question," he said. "What about the girl? Edna?"

Luceile shook her head. "What girl?"

Mr. Blake frowned. "The girl. Edna. Their granddaughter."

"Granddaughter?" Luceile repeated.

"Yes, the boy's sister. Darren and Sandrine's granddaughter. Where will she be during this fantastic lunch on Sunday?"

"Why, Paul. The granddaughter was killed in the car accident with the mother. You know that."

Mr. Blake stiffened. "No."

"Yes, dear. Remember? Sandrine was preparing a little red sundress to send to the child for the summer when the accident happened. The girl was buried in it, as I recall," Luceile said.

Mr. Blake closed his eyes. And saw Omaha. Laughing.

"I saw the girl," he said.

"Oh no, Paul. We never met the little girl. Just Omaha. You know that Darren and Sandrine had been estranged from their daughter before the accident."

He opened his eyes and looked at his wife. "I saw the girl today," he said.

Luceile's face drooped, and she squeezed his hands. "No, Paul."

"I saw her."

Luceile tried to lead him away from the door into the kitchen, but he remained planted in the hallway. Her face was tacked with worry.

"It's my fault. I haven't been making sure you've been taking your medicine... Oh, Paul. Dr. Thatcher seemed so sure that the delusions would pass," she murmured, feeling his forehead again.

Mr. Blake's face tightened in indignation. "I'm not crazy, Ceile."

"Of course not, dear," she said gently. "Come and sit down. I'll make you some breakfast."

Mr. Blake pulled out of her light grasp and flung the front door open. Dashing out onto his porch, he charged down the steps like he was rushing out to face the Japanese until he stood beside a puddle in the rain. He stared at his own sallow reflection.

"Paul!" Luceile called from the porch.

He ignored her and continued to stare at the tiny pool of water. Gritting his teeth, he stepped gingerly on the water's edge and stepped back. Sucking in a gust of courage, he balled his hands at his sides, closed his eyes, and took a determined step into the puddle.

Behind his eyes, he saw Omaha. Laughing.

Beneath his feet, he felt the squishing foundation of mud as his shoes were buried in the shallow body of water.

Opening his eyes, he looked up towards the sky and allowed the tears that were welling up in his eyes to escape down his face. Luceile hurried off the porch and over to her husband.

"Paul, come inside," she said.

He looked at her with absolute sorrow in his eyes. "I can't do it," he said.

Luceile placed a gentle hand on his arm. "It's OK," she said.

He moaned. "Ceile, it's not OK--I'm not OK," he said. He brushed her fingers off his arm. "Just leave me be a minute."

Luceile reluctantly stepped backwards towards the house, her face masked in years' worth of worry. Mr. Blake stared at his reflection in the puddle and kicked the water to kill his distorted image. Shivering in the warm rain, he turned and walked slowly towards his wife.

"Every year, we plow our field, plant a new crop, wait for it to grow," he said, standing face-to-face with Luceile. "Every year, we roll a new leaf over, a new life over, a new love over. That's a natural cycle, right, every year, right?" He paused and glanced up at the thick clouds. "Something is wrong with me, Ceile. Because I can't walk on water, not anymore."

"Paul, no one is asking you to walk on water," Luceile said.

"I feel like I'm back in the war -- that maybe it never ended." Mr. Blake clutched his wife close to his body and sobbed. Closing his eyes, he saw Omaha. Laughing. Opening them, he turned and faced Deetz' house. He saw Omaha standing alone on the porch. Smiling and waving.

"Hey Mr. Blake!" he called. "Looks like the clouds beat the weatherman today!"

Mr. Blake stared across the street at the boy and said nothing as the rain pounded down on his sunburned head.

Victory

*Hold your breath and ease your mind*
*"Four Days"*

She drove an average of ten miles an hour over the speed limit. The fast lane was an unpredictable place to travel but it was the only route she knew. Spinning the dial on her radio, she cranked the music and belted out popular tunes, unpopular tunes, old and new, a voice only a mother could criticize, and ignored the others on the road. She drove the way she wanted to drive, she always had.

She left Louis, her current loser, on a Tuesday and had been traveling for the last four days backwards in time towards the hub of her memories. The road was familiar to her, and she felt a certain degree of possessiveness as she glided along the outskirts of white lines and pale cement. Her mind flashed to her brother's favorite movie -- *Robin Hood, Prince of Thieves* starring the loathsome Kevin Costner -- and Robin's savage pleasure returning to England. He had leapt from the boat and stuck his face in the slimy, cold sand on the beach. She smiled and wondered if she should raise a few eyebrows on the interstate by throwing her emergency brake and sprawling herself on the cement.

"Welcome home, Dorrie," she said, winking at her reflection in the rearview mirror. "It's nice to be back."

Settling back in her seat, she crooned along with Nirvana and ignored the fact that "Age 40" flashed in her rearview mirror. She watched the road signs blink by her faster than the days of her life -- Chelsea Road, Silver Pond and Dees Avenue, Smith Road, and, finally, Cumbers-Manning. Hers. Her hands rested tightly around the steering wheel as she listened to the morning drivel of the DJs.

"Play a motivational song," she said to her radio. "Quit yapping."

"This is an interesting story, Jeff," one of the DJs said in a clappy, high-pitched voice. "A farmer in Holmes County was supposed to be honored at some veterans memorial but he cracked up and bailed on the ceremony."

"What do you mean he cracked up?" Jeff asked.

"I guess he started telling people that his neighbor's grandson could walk on water..."

"That's messed up," Jeff said.

Doreen turned the dial to another setting. "Kid can walk on water? Let him drop a line my way." Her eyes flashed up towards the sky. "I can use all the divine interventions I can get." She bit her lip nervously and cruised down the exit ramp. Her foot rested on the brake as she clutched the wheel. It was seven-thirty in the morning and no one waited behind her.

"Right....right....right...." she murmured. Breathing deeply, she gunned it right and sped off down Cumbers-Manning.

Almost. There.

At her light, she turned left instead of right and cruised past the early-morning golfers. She went the speed limit and sucked in the richness of the towering houses lining the road. Watching a ball hook sharply to the right, she winced as it landed on the patio of one of the giant homes.

"The luxurious homes on the back nine," she mumbled. "Live where your windows can be broken on a daily basis."

She drove to the Bob Evans three miles out of her way and sat in the parking lot, her hands still gripping the steering wheel. The parking lot was half-full, and she wished she knew which cars belonged to regulars and which belonged to outsiders like herself. Her stomach rumbled, and she loosed her grip on the wheel. Glancing at her reflection in the dusty mirror, she pulled her lipstick out of her purse and painted the blush-red color on her tired lips. Running her fingers through her long, bleached-blond hair, she closed her eyes and opened her door. She walked across the parking lot as if she were supposed to be there, supposed to be meeting someone, supposed to absolve that four day's distance with a plate of pancakes and a glass of orange juice.

Once inside, she was ushered to a small table in the back, next to a window. She could feel the eyes of the regulars on her as she stared at the menu without reading it. A waitress appeared by her side and, without looking at her, asked for her order.

"Coffee and a cheese omelet," Doreen said to the waitress' down-turned face.

"Sure thing," the waitress said, vanishing as quickly as she'd come. She brought out her food in short order and left her alone.

Grasping the coffee cup in her slightly wrinkled hand, Doreen drew a deep breath and blew a gust of steam away from her face. She stared at the omelet and thought about breaking some eggs.

"I should call Steve," she said to her food.

She put down her coffee cup and ambled over to the pay phone near the door. Shaking a quarter loose from her pocket, she plunked the coin into the chute and dialed her brother's number. It rang eight times before...

"*What* in God's *holy* hell do you *want* at *eight* in the *morning*?"

Laughing, she pressed her hand against the wall. "Stevie? Were you sleeping?"

There was a long pause. "Dorrie?"

She couldn't read his tone. "Yeah, yeah, it's me."

Another pause.

"Steve, I--"

"Dor, are you in town?"

"Right now, I'm at Bob Evans," she said.

"Are you going to try to see Mom?"

She smiled sadly. "Gee, Stevie, you almost say that like I shouldn't try to see the old bitch."

"Don't start, Dor."

"Don't talk to me like I don't have a reason."

Pause. "Stay there. I'm coming to meet you."

Before she could respond, the dial tone was blaring in her ear. She felt the insides of her cool cover begin to tremble. She turned and nonchalantly moved back to her table where she resumed blowing on her hot, black coffee. The waitress swung by to see how she was doing, and she requested another cup of coffee and a short stack of pancakes for Steve. The food was waiting for him when he walked through the door.

He looked older than she remembered. His once buoyant smile was replaced by a wary grimace, the once round and babied cheeks were stubbled and sagging, the sandy hair was thinning and receding. His athletic frame proved that he still cared enough to work out, but his gait was forced and deliberate instead of flashy and playful. She smiled, though, when she saw her big brother.

"Thought you might be hungry." She waved her long plastic nails at the pancakes.

"Doreen, cut the shit," he said as he sat down.

She held up her knife. "Why don't you cut it for me."

He stared at her. "You look like hell," he said.

She set the knife down and leaned back in her chair. "Fifteen years go by and all you can say is, 'You look like hell.'" She snorted. "You don't exactly look like Casanova, either, sweetie."

"Did you get a nose job or something?" he asked.

She frowned. "I got new boobs. Can we move on?"

He raised an eyebrow. "Which one bought you boobs? Dave? Ricky? Ellis? Carl? Or the new guy -- what's his name? Leo?"

"Louis. And I was joking."

He looked at her skeptically.

"OK. Ricky bought me the nose. Will you give it a rest now?"

He half-grinned at her. "It's been a long time, Dorrie. New nose or not."

She nodded. "I'm sorry about that, Stevie, I really am."

He eyed her. "Carolyn was here a few days ago."

She looked away. "Really."

"Yeh, Dor. She asked about you. Wondered where you were... Wondered if you'd show up to see Mom. We laid money on it. And guess what -- she won."

"I'm happy to help her out," she mumbled.

Steve picked up his fork and began to cut his pancakes. "She loves you, Dor. She really does."

"Who? Carolyn or Mom?"

Steve paused with his fork in midair. "Carolyn, Dor. Carolyn really misses you."

She sighed and her insides quaked. "I know. I'm the worst sister in the world. My baby sister and my older brother are happy to remind me of my failings... And my mother pretends I don't exist."

He began to chew. "She hasn't forgotten you, Dor."

She sniffed. "No, I'd guess that she'd remember me quite well."

"Are you going to try to see her?"

She looked him dead in the eyes. "That's why I'm here, Steve. I came to see that woman before she headed off to hell."

He nodded. "I figured you'd say as much. I was just hoping..."

"Hoping what? That you could convince me to stay away? You knew I'd come when you sent me that letter..."

"She's your mother, Dor. I had to let you know that she was dying, no matter how you feel about her. And I was hoping that you would either dig some good will out of your heart and come to say good-bye or you'd do your victory dance behind your own door. I didn't send you that letter so you could come here and battle an old demon."

She smiled. "I'm not here to hold that bitch's hand."

His fork clattered against his plate. Folding his hands beneath his chin in a tight ball, Steve narrowed his eyes in on hers. "Let it go, Dor."

"Did she let it go?"

He shook his head and looked out the window. Sighing, he stood up. "Thanks for the pancakes, Dor. Don't let it be another fifteen years before we have breakfast together again."

She watched him smack the door with his flat palm. Leaning back in her chair, she wished for the strength to go after him, to make him understand. But she knew he already did understand.

She finished her coffee in one gigantic gulp and signaled for her check. It was almost nine. Heading back out to her worn Accord, she leaned against the driver's side door and contemplated her next move. She knew Steve would probably call their mother. Now she could ease her way back into her mother's life, like the cancer that ate slowly away at the lining of her mother's stomach. She smiled and got into her car.

She drove across the street to a motel and paid cash for one night. The desk attendant gave her the keys to a room on the second floor. She went up, carting her own duffel bag. Flopping on the cheap blue and tan bedspread, she sucked in the motel smell of clean and grinned at the plaster on the ceiling. She was a patient predator; she would bide her time until the right moment to strike presented itself.

She spent the day in the motel, watching her soap operas and tuning into some of the trashy talk shows. She tried to avoid the talk shows because on more than one occasion, old acquaintances of hers had appeared as guests, and she hated to admit that her comrades were on the Jerry Springer-level.

In the evening, she grew restless. Standing at the mirror in the motel bathroom, she stared at her reflection and half-wondered how she'd never been a guest on *Ricki Lake* or *Jenny Jones* herself. Her bleached hair sagged below her shoulders, and her roots were inept at hiding her true dark hair color. Deeply tanned, her face was already fairly wrinkled and the despised double chin wiggled slightly as she swallowed. She always wore too much make-up, had since she was in high school. Her lipstick was always a loud pink or red, her cheeks brushed brightly with blush, her eyes lathered with electric eye shadow and plenty of mascara. She was skinny but lacked toning, so her stature was weak. Staring at herself in the mirror, she almost decided to get into her car and drive four days back to Louis, who didn't care about how much war paint she used.

"Desperate times..." she muttered, stripping out of her clothes.

She jumped into the shower and scrubbed her body from head to foot. Standing with the water pouring over her, she turned and looked at the back of her right forearm. Dozens of chicken-scratch scars blemished the otherwise clear skin. Running her fingers over the tiny marks, each only as long as the tip of a blade, she closed her eyes and tried to focus on why she had come.

When she had received the letter from Steve four days ago, she had locked herself in the bathroom and sobbed. Louis had beat his fist on the door and demanded to know what the hell her problem was. She stopped crying when she was ready, opened the bathroom door, and told Louis she was leaving him. They had only been together for eight months. He had shrugged and changed the channel as she headed out the door. She climbed into her car and drove straight home.

*Home.* The word had an odd ring to it.

Since high school, she had been rootless, living off the supposed kindness of others. Working odd-jobs, waitressing, clerking, answering phones and in other venues of vocation, she had spent years sleeping on the couches of co-workers and bosses, in the beds of boyfriends and strangers. She was a free spirit, always had been, and it was the way she wanted to live. But it meant she had no home except this place, the place where she had been born and raised, the place she had spent her whole life trying to escape.

Standing now in the shower, her hair plastered against her face, she breathed deeply and wished for the strength to face her past; she wished for the strength to face her mother. She wished she knew someone who could walk on water and who could push her across the lake of indigestible circumstances that divided her from her family. Turning the water off, she stepped from the shower and wrapped herself in a thin, white towel. Looking at herself in the mirror, she saw the same person she had seen before, wrinkles and all, but this person's eyes were different.

Sliding into a pair of blue jeans and a plain white T-shirt, she grabbed her belongings and headed out into the mild summer evening. She got into her car and drove three miles in the right direction. Stopping in front of a small, gray house, she jumped out of the car almost faster than she could turn off the engine and ran up to the porch. She banged her fist on the plain, black door and waited. Her wet hair dripped down her back.

She heard the sound of a dog barking and the sound of slow footsteps approaching the door. A moment later, the door swung open.

"Doreen. Steven said you might be by."

She stood on the porch, her jaw locked. The skinny, slightly hunched gray-haired woman in a bathrobe and slippers had already turned and was heading into the den. The door was left open and her mother's lhasa apso stood with a slight snarl on its lip on the welcome mat.

"Prissy, come."

The dog turned its head toward the old voice and scampered into the den. She stood completely still and waited for her feet to move.

"Goddamn it, Doreen. Close the door and get out if all you're going to do is stand there."

Gritting her teeth, she entered the house and fought the urge to slam the door behind her. She followed the dog's path to the den and stood in the room's doorway. It was dark except for a small table lamp next to the chair where her mother sat. She saw an old family photo sitting on the table beside the lamp. They were all in it, smiling despite their dysfunction.

"So you've come to watch me die, Dorrie? Is that why you're here?"

She moved into the room and sat on the stiff couch across from her mother. She said nothing.

Her mother's sharp green eyes carefully inspected her. "Steven said you looked well. I'd say he was mistaken. Can't you afford a decent pair of pants? Or shoes? Not getting the good tips since you lost your looks?"

She looked away. "Mother, you can say all of the hurtful things that you want. It doesn't change the fact that you're dying."

"Nor does your presence here, but here you are. What do you want, Doreen?" Her mother coughed.

She looked her mother in the eye. "Mother, I came because I had something to tell you. I want to say it and leave."

Her mother shrugged. "So say what you have to say."

She got up and moved towards her. Kneeling on the floor by her mother's chair, she said, "Before Daddy left, you were a hard person to bear -- a harder person to please. But once he was gone... You were downright horrible to me and Stevie. Carolyn, well, she was always your favorite, so be it. When I was a kid, Mama, all I ever wanted was for you to look at me and say, 'Dorrie, I'm proud of you.'" She looked her mother in the eye. "You never said that to me. Not once. And I tried so hard to please you."

"Doreen, you can't possibly still be carrying around this sort of baggage. I was hard on you and your brother because you deserved a swift kick in the butt."

"No, Mama. You were hard on us because Daddy loved us more than he loved you."

Her mother's jaw clenched. "Your father was a drunk and an abuser. If that's the kind of love you're seeking in life, little missy, I think you've done a good job. All I ever wanted was for you to live a better life than me."

"That's a lie, Mother. You wanted me to fail, and you wanted Stevie to fail." She stood up. "And look at us. Both failures, Mama! Both of us!" She put her hands on the arms of her mother's chair and leaned in towards her face. "We're what you trained us to be. We're nothings."

Her mother didn't flinch. "That's right, Doreen. You're nothing. You always were nothing and once I'm dead, you'll continue to be nothing. Steven, though, at least tried to learn a trade when he went to vocational school. But you -- you're nothing but a whore."

Her eyes narrowed. "You think so, Mama? You think I'm a whore? Well, maybe I am. I'm a nothing whore. Right now, the only house I have to stay in is this one, and you know what? I'd rather sleep in the sewer than stay here with you."

"Be careful, Doreen. You might give the sewer rats a disease or two."

She laughed in short staccato breaths. "Four days ago, when I got the letter from Stevie that said you were dying of cancer, I wondered what I should do. Should I bother and come to see that old loveless sack of flesh or should I deny her the pleasure of spitting in my face one last time. And you know what I decided?"

Her mother's eyebrows raised. "What, Doreen?"

"I decided that I would come and spit in yours first. You are a heartless old bitch and I had to come and tell you that before you died. I came to tell you that I turned out just the way you'd hoped I would, pathetic and rootless and poor. I am the whore you promised I'd become. But more than those things, Mother, I am here to tell you that all of your abuse couldn't kill me. After all of these years and all of this discouragement, I am the one still standing. You're the invalid. You're the one about to die. You're the one living a loveless, meaningless life. My life may not be perfect, but at least I'm not a coward. At least I can admit my faults. At least I never allowed myself to stay in a relationship where I was beat up by some drunken loser, like my father. At least I always left them before they could leave me." She paused and stared at the blank look in her mother's eye. Turning towards the door, she said, "Good-bye, Mama. I'm glad that you'll die knowing that you couldn't kill me."

She left through the front door as her mother turned on the TV.

She got into her car and drove out towards the countryside. It was dusk now, almost completely dark. Staring at her hands on the steering wheel, she saw herself began to shake. A sense of panic settled in her stomach, but her foot remained steady on the gas pedal. She drove until there were no more road signs and only fields surrounded her. Clasping her hand over her mouth, she choked back a cry.

"Don't do it..." she moaned. "Don't cry -- not over her."

She slammed her foot on the brakes and jumped out of the car. Only her headlights provided any hint of civilization. The pavement was gritty and dusty and in need of repair. She sat on the gravel shoulder and let the tears fall. The second time in four days that she had cried about her mother.

Suddenly, she heard the cry of a bird as it took off from the center of the tall grains planted in the field. Looking up, she saw the ghost-shadow of a crow clash against the black Ohio sky. Startled from its nest, the bird seemed to soar higher and higher until its shape was barely visible from the ground. Doreen sat very still and watched the bird's retreat as she dried her eyes.

The Caws

*Hey, I only want the same as anyone*
*"Rain King"*


*I want I want I want.*

The air spoke softly as his pick-up truck rumbled over the country road. The night seemed particularly dark, and he whistled slightly to himself as he kept an alert watch out for raccoons or skunks that might be trying to dash across the road. He stopped whistling when he spotted headlights coming in the other direction. As he approached, he realized the car was stationary, and a woman sat on the shoulder nearby. He slowed and rolled his window down.

"Evening ma'am. Are you OK? Car trouble?" he asked.

She had been crying. "No, I'm fine. Thank you, though."

He hesitated until something in her eyes made him realize that she didn't need his help, and he nodded. "I live in the house across this field. Feel free to come and knock."

She stood and brushed the gravel off of herself. "You're very kind. Thank you."

He offered a smile and rolled his window up. As he drove on towards his driveway, he saw her get into her car and drive away before he pulled onto the dirt road that led to his family's house.

The house was a magnificent thing to look at, even in the dark. It was one of the larger farm houses in Manning Township and had been in his family for three generations. Three stories tall, the white house with four pillars had been dubbed the Caw Manse by their neighbors. The first to live in the house was Reverend Jimmy Caw and his wife Silk, and they had left the house to their only son Reverend Jimmy Caw and his wife Bella. When Jimmy and Bella decided to move to Arizona, they had turned the property over to their only son Jimmy Caw and his wife Lily.

*I want I want I want.*

Jimmy's truck left a cloud of dust and dirt in its wake as he pulled up by the barn. Jumping out, he whistled as he unloaded the few bags of horse feed from the bed. Swinging open the red door of the barn, he dragged the bags inside. He paused to light the lantern and then checked on his two mares, Betty and Cassy. When he was satisfied that everything was settled in the barn, he extinguished the lantern and locked the door behind him. Looking up at his house, he saw that Lily's light was still on. He smiled, imagining her soft brown hair resting on her shoulders, her eyes opening as she heard him come in her room. She would smile when she saw him and whisper for him to come to her. Jimmy felt a warmth spread through his body, and he bolted in the front door.

His wife's basset hound Spaghetti lay by the door. "Hey, boy," he said, scratching the dog's head. "Where's mama?"

Spaghetti looked up at him with droopy brown eyes and yawned. Jimmy grinned and ran up the master staircase, two steps at a time. His wife's door was closed, but the light still filtered out into the hallway. He licked his fingers and smoothed back his hair before knocking twice, softly.

"Come in, Jimmy," the voice said.

He opened the door slowly and entered the room. Lily's nurse Clara sat in the wooden rocking chair he had built for his wife on their first anniversary. She set down the book she'd borrowed off Lily's expansive shelf and smiled at him. He smiled back.

"How is she tonight?" he asked, his eyes fixed on his sleeping wife.

Clara's eyes were calm. "Fine, dear. She was having some pain while you were gone. I've given her some morphine."

Jimmy sat on the edge of his wife's bed and took her hand into his own. "Oh."

Clara got up from the chair and put her hand on Jimmy's shoulder. "Let's talk downstairs, OK?"

He leaned over and kissed his wife's nose. "Sure, Clara."

She left the lamp on in Lily's room and the two of them went down a back staircase that led to the kitchen. Sitting across the plain oak table he had made as a teenager, Clara seemed more somber than usual. They said nothing for a moment and the silence made Jimmy fidget in his seat.

"I need some lemonade. Want any?" he asked, moving toward the oversized refrigerator.

"Sure, dear," Clara said with a sigh.

He opened the refrigerator and grabbed the glass pitcher from the midst of stacks of white boxes. "Was she baking today?" he asked, pouring them each a glass.

"The Murphy-Slate wedding is this week," Clara said. "I told her maybe she shouldn't offer to take on such large orders anymore."

His eyes clouded. "Let her do what she wants. You aren't here to boss her around -- you're here to make her better."

She got up from the table and stood behind him. She was far shorter than he, 5'2" to his 6'5", but she reached up and put her hand on his shoulder anyway. "You know she's not getting better, Jimmy."

His shoulders sagged, and he had to steady himself with both hands lying flat on the countertop. "I know."

She picked the lemonade up off the counter and guided him back over to the table. "She told me today that she wants to go to the live-in hospice."

Clara's voice was calm and even. He stared at his glass of lemonade. "She wants to leave me? Leave here?"

"She thought it would be easier for you."

He swallowed hard and fought back bitter laughter. "I don't think anything would make this easier."

"I told her that I would let you know her wishes. But, Jimmy, if I were you, I'd try and persuade her to stay. She loves this house and you and that silly old dog. She'd be better off here."

Jimmy sat motionless. Head in his hands, he said, "I saw a woman by the side of the road tonight who I stopped to help because I thought she was in trouble." He paused and looked at Clara. "But she got in her car and drove away and didn't need my help. I offered her what I could, and she was thankful and humble and kind. But she didn't need me. She was strong enough on her own."

"Lily isn't that woman, Jimmy. Not now."

"No. But she used to be that woman, strong and independent. She wants to leave me because she still wants to be that person." He looked at her. "Should I really tell her she can't be?"

"Yes," Clara said.

Jimmy stood up. "I'm going to bed," he said. He left Clara alone at the table with the two untouched glasses of lemonade and ran up the back stairs. He went into his wife's room and, still in his clothes, curled up next to her. His eyes fixed on Lily's dog-eared copy of Saul Bellow's *Henderson the Rain King*. Her favorite novel.

*I want I want I want.*

As the sun rose the next morning, he was already out in the field. He worked the land himself with the help of a few of the local boys. It was Sunday, though, so he was out there alone. He worked quickly and moved to the barn. He let the horses out to graze and swept their stalls. He cleaned out the rabbit hutches and tended the goats.

Unlike his father and grandfather, he had not found a holy calling for ministry. He liked to work with his hands and enjoyed the dirt under his fingernails, the sweat caking his body. When he wasn't working on the farm, he was in his wood shop adjacent to the barn. His life's ambition was building furniture, but in all reality he had inherited enough money to live comfortably the rest of his life pursuing no vocation whatsoever. When he and Lily had gotten married three years ago, they had merged two fairly substantial family fortunes, but they had agreed that active lives were the most fulfilling. So Jimmy had installed his wood shop and Lily had revamped the Caw Manse kitchen into a state-of-the-art cooking facility. They put all of their earnings away in a special bank account for their son Jimmy.

*I want I want I want.*

Jimmy leaned against the barn door and looked up towards his wife's window. Breathing deeply, he wondered what he'd do with all of the money for a little Jimmy who was never conceived, never born. A year after they were married, Lily began to have trouble breathing and would experience chest pains. After an especially bad attack, Jimmy had rushed his bride to the hospital where the first of a long string of doctors diagnosed her with the onset of congenital heart failure at age twenty-two. Lily had wanted them to try and have a child soon after they accepted she was sick, but Jimmy had refused her. Up until then, it was the only time he refused her anything.

"Pregnancy could kill you," he'd said. "Let's fight this and beat it. Then we'll have as many children as you want."

She had smiled at him, but her eyes were sadder than he'd ever seen them. "I want that, Jimmy."

Two months ago, when Clara had moved in with them, Lily had taken Jimmy's hand and said, "When I'm gone, I want you to save the money for the baby. Because someday you'll have him, and I want to be able to give him something."

Jimmy felt his knees weaken, and he sank to the dusty ground. He could feel the tears well up in his throat. He'd never have that child.

*I want I want I want.*

"Jimmy! Come here, quick!"

His head shot up and he saw Clara waving frantically at him from the front porch. He bolted to the house and leapt up the steps. He could hear Spaghetti howling. Clara grabbed him by the arm and dragged him to the kitchen where Lily sat at the table. She was breathing heavily, but she was smiling. The dog kept howling.

"Lil, are you OK?" he asked, his eyes wide and startled.

She laughed. "Yes, yes, of course. 'ghetti, shhh..." She placed a weak hand over the hound's eyes.

Jimmy looked from Clara to his wife. "What's going on?"

"I wanted to show you what I made for you," Lily said, breathing deeply.

Clara grinned and nudged him over to the oven. "Open it and see."

Numbly, he did as he was told, his eyes remaining on his wife. As he pulled the oven door open, his nostrils awoke to the scent of banana nut bread. His favorite. He slid his hands into potholders and pulled the pan out. He set it on top of the stove and moved over to his wife, kissing her on top of her head.

"Thanks, Lily. But, you, Clara," he said, shooting her a look, "you should not be yelling at me like that. I thought there was something wrong, I thought...."

Lily reached up and grabbed his hand. "Nothing was wrong, Jimmy. Just come and sit here by me a little."

Clara smiled. "I'll be upstairs, if you need me."

Lily brushed her pale fingers over his sweat-streaked face. "Clara told me she spoke to you about the hospice."

Jimmy gritted his teeth. "She did."

Lily tilted her head. "But you don't approve?"

"How could I approve of you moving away from me? That's why we hired Clara -- to bring the hospice to you."

"I just don't want this house to remind you of my death."

"Oh, Lily. When I think of this house, I will always think of you."

She smiled and looked him in the eye. "Why don't you cut a piece of that bread for yourself, and one for Spaghetti, too."

"I don't mind if I do," he said, feeling nearly happy.

"Can I ask you a question?" she asked as he stood up.

"Sure, Lil. Anything."

"What do you think Heaven is like?"

He turned his head towards her as he cut the bread. "My grandfather used to say heaven was the Indians in the World Series."

Lily groaned. "A reverend thinks that heaven is a baseball game?"

"Hey," Jimmy said defensively as he set a plate on the ground for the waiting Spaghetti, "not just a baseball game. The World Series."

"So you agree that that's Heaven?" she asked.

"Absolutely," he said with a wide grin.

Her face became serious. "I think Heaven is a place washed clean where new things can begin and where everything can grow and heal. I think Heaven is like a garden where the roses have no thorns and nothing ever wilts. I think Heaven is everlasting and ever true." She turned and took Jimmy's hand. "I think Heaven will be OK. I think I will be OK." She eyed him carefully. "Will you be OK?"

He scratched his head and swallowed thickly. "I *want* to be OK."

She put her arms around him, and he dug his fingers into her shoulder. "God, Lil, don't you think we deserve better? We deserve more time together. My whole life, I've lived by the books. I never got into trouble, I never laid a hurtful hand on anyone... I did everything right, and here we are. Talking about Heaven." He pulled back from her. "I deserve more from Him. I belong in your service, living for you, and He won't let me. I want something better than He seems willing to give me."

She smoothed his hair back. "Jimmy, I love you. But you have to live for yourself." She drew a shallow breath.

He closed his eyes. "My father used to say that souls were taken to Heaven in the belly of a black-winged bird. And I asked him once, why a black bird -- why its belly. You'd think it would be a white bird, and they'd ride on its back." He opened his eyes and cupped her chin in his hand. "He said, 'Jimmy, the Good Lord gets it done, whether the bird is black or white, whether a soul is tucked inside or riding.' Lily, I've accepted that you're going to die, but please don't die alone. Whether you go or stay, you'll die, but if you stay, I can be here to hold you."

*I want I want I want.*

She closed her eyes. "I'll stay."


The next few weeks ambled by at a peaceful pace. Jimmy took his wife on long drives in the countryside, with Spaghetti riding in the bed of the truck. The dog seemed to be growing more and more sensitive to the fact that Lily was deteriorating each day and rarely strayed from her side. The day before she died, Spaghetti spent the better part of the afternoon pacing between Lily and Jimmy, whining and pawing at them. Lily had spent that day in her rocking chair with Jimmy sitting at her feet, helping her write a letter to her family and friends. The letter was a good-bye letter that was streaked with the sweat off Jimmy's hands.

*I want I want I want.*

Early the next morning, Jimmy woke up with a start. Flipping on the bedside lamp, he turned towards his wife. He brushed her hair back from her face and was startled by her coolness. He began to tremble, and he knew. He leaned over her breathless body to kiss her one last time. He saw Spaghetti lying on the floor, his large brown eyes revealing that he knew, also.

Sliding out of bed, he calmly walked to Clara's room and knocked softly. Seconds later, the door flung open to reveal a wide-awake nurse. "She's gone, isn't she."

He closed his eyes. Nodding slowly, she grasped his forearm and walked with him back to Lily's bedroom. Clara examined her and called the hospice to inform them of the passing. He blinked and felt numb. When the ambulance came to take the body away, he barely even registered the hospice workers' presence. Clara had sat by him and said nothing. When the hospital equipment was removed from the Caw Manse, Clara began making phone calls, first to Lily's parents and then Jimmy's. Within twenty-four hours, the house was full of friends and family, but Jimmy didn't even know they were there. A continuous stream of *"She'll be missed"* filled his ears.

"Jimmy, we loved her, too," said an old friend.

"Miss who?" he'd said.

After the funeral, the dust from the stampede of visitors settled, and he was alone with his parents. Clara had moved out, his parents had temporarily moved in. Jimmy settled back into his routine of managing the farm and working in his wood shop. Spaghetti became his shadow. Lily's mother had wanted to take Spaghetti to town with her and Lily's father, but Jimmy had quietly refused.

*I want I want I want.*

One evening in late September, Jimmy and his father walked around the farm with Spaghetti. As they talked, Jimmy could feel a twinge of normalcy in their easy conversation. He glanced at his father sideways.

"Dad, do you remember when you told me about the black-winged bird that took souls to Heaven?"

His father grinned. "Sure, son, of course."

"Isn't that a weird concept for a reverend to believe in?"

"I don't think it's weird to believe that something as beautiful as a bird is the earthly connector to Heaven."

Jimmy stopped walking. "Did I cry at Lily's funeral?"

His father put a strong arm around his son's shoulder. "No, Jimmy."

Jimmy looked at his father. "I don't feel anything, Dad."

"No, son. I suspect you feel too intensely."

"I want to remember her better, but I don't know how. And all I want to do is cry, but I can't." He paused. "How do I fix that?"

His father shook his head. "Son, I wish I could tell you."

A week later, his parents got on the airplane and returned to their lives in Arizona. His first night alone in the house, Jimmy sat at the kitchen table with a bottle of tequila. He had Lily's copy of *Henderson, the Rain King* lying in front of him. One of the last things she touched before she left him. Staring at the worn cover, he swallowed thickly and poured himself a shot. Tipping his head back, he downed the burning liquid and shook away the pain. He picked up the book and thumbed through the pages. He'd never read it, even though Lily had told him and told him and told him that he should take the time. He'd grinned and told her if Eugene Henderson could make a side table faster than he could, it might be worth his time.

"Eugene only makes a mess of things," she'd said.

Sitting at the kitchen table with the book in front of him, he chewed on Lily's words as he poured another shot. His head was already swimming. Opening the book, he choked on his wife's neat handwriting in the margins, choked on the first underlined passage he came across:

*"Grief has kept me in condition and that's why this body is so tough."*

Jimmy ground his fists into his eye sockets and willed himself to cry. Willed himself to knock down his own wall. Willed himself to clang the bell of grief in his brain.

*"I have never been able to convince myself that the dead are utterly dead."*

Eugene Henderson's words leaking out of Jimmy's pores. Eugene Henderson, the Rain King, the man who made a mess of everything. The man who lived by the mantra of *"I want I want I want..."* Jimmy closed his eyes and tried to scream, but he couldn't.

*"Maybe I have kissed life too hard and weakened the structure."*

He wanted to tear the book to pieces, rip Eugene Henderson limb from limb. Rip the pain in his disjointed soul out through his mouth and slip it into a Tupperware container to be stored in the now largely empty refrigerator. In *her* kitchen. He wanted it all to end.

*"Everyone should study the Bible."*

He hated the Bible. Hated God, still, for ignoring the generations of his family who had lived to walk in the shadow of His greatness, preaching His word. He hated the fact that God didn't care what he wanted, didn't care how much he was hurting. Didn't care that he needed Lily, as much as Henderson needed his own wife Lily.

"You and Henderson have at least that in common," Lily had teased him.

Jimmy didn't want to have anything in common with Henderson the Rain King. He traced his fingers along his dry, tense face and wondered if he should be known as Jimmy the Drought King.

*"But there comes a day, there always comes a day of tears and madness."*

Jimmy threw the book at the refrigerator and wondered, wondered when that day would come for him. He closed his eyes and saw Eugene Henderson's fictional mouth twitch in anticipation.

A month later, Jimmy and Spaghetti had settled into yet another routine in their quest to establish life after Lily. One afternoon, Jimmy got a card from his father with a ink drawing of a crow across the front. It said, *"Dear Jimmy, Maybe it's time for you to go and talk to her. Say good-bye. She'll understand, son."*

Jimmy propped the note up on his dresser, while Spaghetti lay at his feet, yawning. He had never been to the cemetery, not since the burial. Glimpsing the faded copy of *Henderson the Rain King*, now back on the bookshelf, he wondered if it was time.

*"You have a specific job to do,"* Henderson whispered from the pages.

Late that afternoon, Jimmy got into his truck and drove into town to visit his wife. He found the site easily; her mother tended it weekly. Standing at the head of the grave in the chilly October air, he stared at the headstone. *Lily Robinson Caw, Beloved Wife and Daughter.* He blinked. Lily Robinson Caw. He knelt on the slightly damp ground and twirled a leaf between his thumb and forefinger.

"Hi. I mean, hello. Lily." He paused to clear his throat. "I'm sorry I haven't been to see you. God, I just miss you so much." He shook his head. "There are days I feel like lying down in the field and surrendering myself to God. Let the black-winged bird come and collect me. All I know is that I shouldn't have to miss you." Another pause. "I got drunk the other night to see if I could feel anything but all that I felt was hatred for my drinking buddy, Eugene Henderson. I thought I'd get to know him since he was a friend of yours, but I hated everything he had to say because he sounded like me. Too much like me." He stood up. "I came here to get your permission to feel again."

Standing with his hands crossed in front of his chest, he watched the leaves blow across the grave marker. Suddenly, a small voice beside him said, "Mister, wanna buy a flower for the grave?"

Looking, he saw a young girl, maybe ten years old, standing with a basket of white roses. He picked one up and examined it. "No thorns," he said.

"They're only a dollar, mister."

*I want I want I want.*

He handed the girl a dollar from his pocket and clutched the rose in his fist.

Just Like a Woman

*We couldn't all be cowboys*
*So some of us are clowns*
*And some of us are dancers on the midway*
*We roam from town to town*
        *"Goodnight, Elisabeth"*

He sat in a stupor on a cracking green bench. Large gray and white splotches speckled the wooden frame, and he rested his thumbs on dime-size bare spots. It was early afternoon, but his eyes were already wide-shut, and he was drifting somewhere high above the town. The only thing that grounded him was the graveyard across the street and the five o'clock bus that was due any moment. He stared through the black wrought-iron fence of the cemetery and narrowed his eyes on a tall, awkward-looking man with a young girl. He half-stood when he saw the white flower in the man's hand. A rose. Not a daffodil. He sat back down.

Lenny, a black man wearing a thick, green jacket with "City Grounds Crew" embroidered across the front, walked down the street to where he was sitting. He smiled and laughed when he saw his old co-worker planted on the bench.

"My man, what's up?" Lenny asked.

He smiled and rolled his lips over his gums to reveal tobacco-stained teeth. "Some of nothing," he said.

Lenny guffawed. "Damn, I still think you should write a book of your sayings."

He pursed his cracked lips. "Maybe someday I will."

"Say, we could use you back on the crew. The fellas miss you, man. If you're ever interested, all you gotta do is stop by the office," Lenny said.

He shook his head and squinted. "Elisabeth keeps me pretty busy these days."

Lenny's exuberance faded. "I see."

He closed his eyes and still saw Lenny's down turned smile. "Thanks, though."

Lenny shrugged. "Suit yourself, man, OK? Take care."

"I'll try to remember to do that," he mumbled. Shaking his head, he turned his attention back across the street. The man and the girl were gone. He sighed and wondered what sort of trouble was in store for him behind the wrought iron fence that separated the living from the nonliving. An ironic smile twisted his lips as he wondered what good the gate really was. He thought of the dead bodies he'd seen dangling from tree branches, bodies clothed in black pajamas and tire sandals, bodies staring down at him with youthful, vacant eyes. Dying for a cause. He choked on the image of the flying carcasses as he stared across the street at proper burials and wondered which he'd prefer. Instead of thinking about it more, he lay down on the bench to wait for the bus.

The day was cool, and the sun was playing peek-a-boo through some thick fall storm clouds. The moment he put his head on the bench, the sun crept out from hiding and danced across his eyelids.

"Son of a..." he muttered, pulling his fisherman's hat off and putting it over his face.

Moments later, a light snore fluttered through his lips, and he was alive again. Elisabeth stood beside him, her soft laughter displacing the image of the flying dead. He listened to her hum above the rush of the traffic, the most soothing sound he knew besides the thumping of huey propellers. She was playing with her long, black hair. She hadn't had it cut since she was fourteen, and it stretched down her back. Her violet almond-shaped eyes glowed mischievously as she thumbed some of the long strands. Her body was slouched and seductive, playful almost. She smiled at him with wide, full lips, concealing her teeth to make him forget about her overbite, and squinted her eyes in a most devilish way. *Were you waiting for me?* she asked. *I hope you weren't waiting long.*

The sound of the bus' squeaking breaks jolted him awake, and he sat up in a panic. Wishing for the cold sweat of a broken nightmare, he looked around feverishly for the reality that existed only behind his eyelids. He forgot he was on Earth, not *her* Earth, and blinked his eyes desperately to see if he could see her, find her, hold her once more. His eyes gravitated to the spot, the very place on the sidewalk, where she had just been. *Just been.* He needed her to be there this time, really be there, because he was tired of waking up alone from his nightmares. He grabbed the arm of a woman walking by.

"Did you see her go? Where is she?" His bloodshot eyes were wide with panic.

The woman, startled, shook her arm free and hustled away. "I didn't see anyone, sir."

The bus driver sat behind the wheel and yawned. "Honey, you getting on or are you accosting people today?"

He stared at the person behind the voice, who was tapping her long, neon green plastic nails against the steering wheel. "Keep your weave on, lady, I'm coming. I was just looking for..."

She cracked her orange gum. "Your brains? Honey, I know you fried those long, long ago. Now get your skinny white ass on the bus before I leave you standing there with your mouth open."

He bowed his head sheepishly and did as he was told. He sat in his usual seat, three behind the driver; no one else was on the bus. He stared out the window at the cold, unfriendly gravestones and, fingering his tarnished silver dog tags, felt glad that he hadn't decided to slink through that jungle. Vietnam had taught him not to fight any war that couldn't be won. He settled back in his seat and rested his chin on the thin strip of metal beneath the window. He remained the only passenger until they got to the fringe of town when a young, edgy blond got on with two ordinary looking men. The bus rumbled out through the countryside and onto the interstate. The late-afternoon traffic was as lazy as the orange barrels still lining the right lane. He never budged during the entire trip, not even when the blond had said hello on her way past him to the back of the bus. Instead, he stared at the cars zooming around them and wondered why anyone bothered to pay car insurance when the bus would take you any earthly place you wanted to go.

*"What about transcendental destinations?"* Elisabeth whispered in his ear. *"How many bus tokens does it take to exit the earth?"*

The bus teetered off the exit at Baton Rouge Bridge Road, and he cracked his jaw. His stop. He stood and moved jerkily to the front where he offered the driver -- Lucinda, according to the plate above her on the bus interior -- a smile.

"Take it easy, doll," he said with a wink. "Even chiseled-from-crystal beauties like yourself can play too hard and break too early."

Lucinda rolled her eyes. "Whatever you say, honey. I'll see you next week."

He pressed his hand against his chest in mock horror. "Not tomorrow?"

"Honey, you know I drive the Eastside bus every day but today. You'll see Estes tomorrow."

"But she's not nearly as pretty as you, doll..."

Lucinda laughed. "Save it, honey, really. And do me a favor."

"Anything for you," he said.

The other three passengers stared at the friendly banter with no expression.

"Promise me you will take your own advice and behave yourself."

He smiled and looked away. "I'll see you next week."

He got off the bus and saluted at the retreating hunk of metal. Turning on his heels, he walked across the street without regard to the traffic and headed through a back ally to the side entrance of a motel kitchen. Knocking twice, he waited for the door to creak open. When it did, a short, balding man wearing all white opened the door and grinned.

"Ah, it's the *gringo*. As predictable as a Spanish whore." The man handed him a styrofoam plate with a turkey sandwich on it and pushed him out into the dining room.

The dining room was dimly lit and almost vacant. The only patrons were two elderly gentlemen, a pair who spent the better part of the day playing gin-rummy with tourists in the lobby. Hustlers. He nodded in their direction and sat by himself at a table by the mustard-yellow wall. His chair was wobbly, but he didn't mind. The man from the kitchen came out with a glass of water. Setting it before him, the man slid into the chair across the table.

"Alvin is gone for the day, so take your time and eat."

"You still getting in trouble with your boss?"

"Listen, he knows that you don't ever pay for your food. That draft-dodger hippy doesn't have any respect for you Vietnam vets. Not even now. He's more bitter about life than a woman. If he finds out I'm still feeding you for free, I'll just have him take it out of my paycheck. My brother was killed in 'Nam, so it's the least I can do for one of his jungle buddies."

"Hey, Pablo. Can you get me something a little more potent than lemonade from the bar?"

Pablo looked across the dining area to one of the hustlers, holding his innocent glass of lemonade in the air. "Sure, Gramps. Give me a minute."

The hustler set his glass down and nodded.

"Guy thinks because he's been coming here since before the building was built that he can boss me around," Pablo muttered. Grinning, he slapped his hand on the table. "Eat up, *gringo*. I'll bring you, what, *una cerveza*? Might as well get an early start to keep up with Gramps over there."

He nodded. "Sure. A beer is fine."

Pablo jumped from his seat and ran across the room to retrieve the old man's glass. He sat and watched the hustlers squabble over their small stack of wrinkled bills and felt a pang of pity for the fools those two buzzards had eaten alive that day.

"They make the VC seem like OK folks..." he said to his sandwich.

Moments later, Pablo returned from the bar adjacent to the dining area and set a glass down in front of each of the men. Turning, he backtracked towards the remote table against the mustard-yellow wall. Setting a beer down, he rolled his eyes.

"That old man has an odd taste in alcohol -- that's whiskey and tang. Sick, eh?"

"Yeah, sick," he said as he stuck his finger into his beer and sucked the liquid off his finger.

Pablo stood awkwardly by the table, his face falling. "You OK, *gringo*? Your trip didn't go so well this morning?"

"It went all right -- until I saw her again."

Pablo sat back down. "Saw who? The girl?"

He looked annoyed. "Yeah, the girl. My girl. Elisabeth."

Pablo nodded in remembrance. "Ohhh. E-*liz*-a-beth."

"No, you twit. E-*lis*-a-beth. With an *s*."

Pablo snorted. "Well, pardon me, *gringo*. E-liz-a-beth-*con-s*. Why don't you ever bring her around here?"

He shook his head slowly. "She does what she wants."

"Ain't that like a woman," Pablo chuckled.

"She's like no woman I've ever known. She saved me when I needed saving the most," he said.

Pablo smiled sadly. "You don't think you need saving now?"

He looked him in the eye. "Not like I did then."

Pablo whistled low. "You been coming here for eight months, *gringo*, and all you ever talk about is the girl, this girl I've never seen."

He took a long swig from his beer glass. "I only ever get to see her when she wants me to see her, and it makes me nuts."

Pablo crossed his arms in front of his chest. "She sounds normal enough. Well, I'd better get back to work. Enjoy your beer."

"Thanks. Just put it on my tab," he said.

Pablo chuckled. "Sure thing, *gringo*. Whatever you say."

The hustlers watched Pablo retreat to the kitchen and then turned their stares towards him.

"Sonny, why don't you come sit with us? Every day you're here, and every day you sit alone."

He responded by getting up and leaving the dining room.

He headed out towards the lobby of the California Motel, named for Clifford California, a locally famous jazz musician who had settled his act in the motel's lounge during its heyday seventy years ago. Now, the city around the building was just as beat-up and worn out as the motel itself. A steady clientele of prostitutes, potheads, and unsuspecting tourists kept the California Motel in business. As he walked down the hall on the worn red and blue checked carpeting, he stopped to look at the photograph of Clifford with his cheeks puffed out like a blow fish as he blazed a crowd-pleasing tune on his brass trumpet. He felt sorry for old Clifford because now people either didn't know who he was or didn't care.

"Hey, baby. There you are. I thought maybe you missed your bus today or something."

He turned and looked toward the voice. It belonged to a skinny female with frizzy brown hair and a narrow face. "Hi, Coreen," he said.

She winked as she moved towards him. Wrapping her arms around his neck, she kissed his flat lips. "Hi yourself, baby," she said.

He smiled and cupped her chin in his hand. "I didn't know you'd be here today."

She laughed and pulled back from him. "I had a feeling you'd like to see me. Was I right, baby?"

He grinned. "Yeah. Say, do me a favor and wait for me upstairs. I have to say hello to my friend and then I'll be up."

"Sure, baby." Coreen breezed past him in the hallway and headed towards the staircase.

He continued to the lobby where he saw the very friend he'd hoped to see. Moving quickly, he approached him and after a brief exchange, his friend left. Feeling suddenly renewed, he dashed back down the hallway and followed the scent of Coreen's imitation-expensive perfume up to Room 213. His room -- a room for which he never paid. He broke in one night and hung a "Do Not Disturb" sign on the door, and no one questioned his presence. His neighbors changed by the hour, and the cleaning service never bothered him. He opened the door and saw Coreen smoking a cigarette and sitting wide-eyed in the corner by the air conditioner. He closed the door behind him and stared at her.

"You OK?" he asked.

"Mmmm..." she murmured, dragging herself to her feet. She moved towards him and slowly traced her fingers around his face and down his chin. Resting her palm on the inner pocket of his oversized coat, she smiled. "Whatcha got?"

He withdrew the small plastic bag full of white powder from his pocket. "A peace offering."

She took the bag from him. "Give peace a chance," she said.

He grinned. "Which piece is that?"

She took the bag from him and staggered into the bathroom. "Dunno, baby. A piece of ass?"

He choked on his laughter as his knees gave way. Sitting on the edge of the bed with no covers, he covered his face with his hands and tried not to close his eyes. Every time he blinked, he saw her face. *E-lis-a-beth-con-s*. He drew a deep breath and felt himself aging with each pathetic gasp for air.

Coreen stumbled out of the bathroom and flopped on the bed next to him. "Pure shit, man. That was some pure shit."

He swallowed the air and felt like throwing up. "Take your clothes off," he said. He closed his eyes.

*"You miss me, baby? Wrap your heart in daffodils and look me up the next time you hit 'Orleans.'"*

Long after Coreen had left, he lay naked on the bed and thought about the time he'd spent in New Orleans. After he was discharged from the army, he wandered through an enigmatic cloud of instability that rendered him homeless with nothing to his name but his silver dog tags and a second-hand acoustic guitar. He forgot how to keep track of time; he forgot how to care. All that mattered to him were the weak chords he could strum on his guitar, peaceful chords that didn't remind anyone of Vietnam or Lyndon Baines Johnson or malarial pills in the shape of Communism. He wanted to spend his life brushing away the pain of war by callusing his fingers and singing quietly with his face towards the ground.

Time began again for him a lifetime after the war when Elisabeth threw the first of many dollars in his hat. He remembered what she smelled like -- fresh orange peels. He never needed to look up when she went by; he already knew what she looked like, knew that she was coming. One day, she grabbed his hand and jarred his eyes from the pavement. She had smiled. *"You could be my brother,"* she'd said, *"and I'd hope someone would take care of him. You could be somebody's brother just as easily as anyone else."* When she'd gotten a job up North, she packed him up with her mahogany coffee table and her collection of Elvis records and promised to make an honest, civilized man out of him yet. Now dusty and uncivilized, he rolled his head lazily to the side and saw his guitar sitting against the wall. A dried daffodil was stuck through the broken strings. He forced his eyes to focus on the ceiling.

Early the next morning, he climbed on the bus and rode away from the California Motel and decay. He arrived at the town square around seven-fifteen and wondered if he shouldn't get back on the bus and ride out to the grounds office. Eight months ago, when his world had crumbled away from him, he quit the job because he quit everything, and now he wasn't so sure he did the right thing.

As soon as he saw the lights flick on, he entered Stan's for his usual cup of coffee. Normally, he sat on a bench and smoked some after that, but he'd spent that money on Coreen. So he was forced to sit on his green bench sober and choke back the bile building in his throat. Every breath was painful.

He hated his pain.

Staring at the black wrought iron gate surrounding the cemetery, he tried to build up the courage to cross the street. The thick clouds above him shuddered with him and a few raindrops fell around him and on him. He pulled his hat down over his eyes and felt his face begin to burn as a few tears blazed down his cheeks.

*It was an old argument between them. "You can't even rescue yourself, Cowboy. How can you rescue a liberated woman like myself?"*

*"I'm nobody's hero. I'm a clown, a bum. I'm the quintessential baby killer. If anyone needs saving, it's me."*

*"Listen to me. No one can save you. Lord knows, I've tried. So many people love you and care about you, but you still act like you're a tightrope walker whose rope is being burned from both ends. How do you ever expect to get off alive?"*

The tears froze, and he wondered if he was even alive. He looked around for signs of his vitality, but his eyes were drawn back to the cemetery. Sighing, he wished she were there; he wasn't ready to say good-bye. He'd never be ready.

He remembered the last time he saw her, shadowed and silhouetted in the doorframe of her bedroom, with her oversized purse dangling from a slouched shoulder. He sat on the floor, high, and watched her smile through the shadows, frown through the grainy cloud of smoke dissipating through the room. *"Good-bye,"* she'd said in an automated voice. He'd laughed.

Sitting on the bench, he balled his fists and rubbed his eyes, longing to erase the seriousness of good-bye. All he wanted was to sleep away the nightmare of good-bye.

"I'd rather say good-night, Elisabeth," he said, his placid eyes fixed across the street. "At least you can wake-up from good-night."

Trust Fall

*For all the things I'm losing*
*I might as well resign myself to try*
*and make a change*
          *"I Wish I Was a Girl"*

It never ceased to amaze Nicholas Finccoli how quickly human beings retracted from daily routine as soon as the air stiffened and began the slow stride towards freezing. As he walked through the midsection of town early that evening, he shook his head at the lack of activity on the usually vibrant square.

"It's a damn ghost town," he muttered.

At the corner of Johnson and Lemmings, he rocked the soles of his shoes on the pavement and pulled the collar of his jacket up to shield part of his face.   Glancing upwards at the sullen storm clouds, he felt a dollop of cynicism creep into his thoughts as he, too, cursed the coming of winter, the death of barbecues and picnics, lazy hours spent by the pool, warm droplets of summer rain.  Suddenly, a large and rather menacing drop of rain pelted his upturned face.

"Even you're spitting on me now?" he asked the sky.  He wiped the drop away before ducking his head and hurrying across the street.

He continued down Lemmings, slowing only when he came to the bus stop. Here, he paused and stared at a bum who lay stretched out and sleeping on the broken green bench.  He was facing the cemetery across the street, and his mouth hung open as he snored audibly.  Nicholas continued by, shaking his head in amazement at this, his one and only example of humanity on his lonely walk home from the office.

He lived in a modest house with a fresh coat of yellow paint that he'd put on himself that past summer.  After emptying his mailbox, he hurried up to the porch and turned his key in the lock.

"Elizabeth! I'm home!"  He shook the raindrops from his coat and hung it on a peg by the door.

The only response was his own echoed voice.

Nicholas slid his shoes off and headed into the kitchen. Flipping on the overhead light, he reached for the coffee filters to brew himself a pot. He turned on the radio mounted over the sink and began to sing along with the latest too-catchy song.

"You're home." The scent of orange peels wafted towards him.

He spun around and attempted to smile at the face behind the voice. "I am."

Elizabeth was leaning against the doorframe. She was wearing the bathrobe he'd gotten her for Christmas before they were engaged. It was a deep blue, plush and fuzzy. Her black hair was in a messy bun on the top of her head, and she had no make up on.

"I just got up," she said.

He felt his smile slowly dissipate. "Oh."

She turned and headed down the dark hallway towards her bedroom. He stared at the space she had occupied and thoughtfully picked his teeth with his tongue. He turned back towards his coffee. It was English Toffee flavored. Her favorite. He poured a cup and sat down at the kitchen table to sort through the mail. Reaching for his reading glasses from the shelf behind him, he opened the first bill with his trout-shaped letter opener. He went through each bill carefully and wrote checks in neat handwriting. When he was through with the bills, he moved to the letters. There were three: one from his mother in Pennsylvania, one from his sister in Vermont, and one from Denise.

Denise.

That bitch.

The one from Denise was for Elizabeth. Nicholas stared at the shaky handwriting on the light blue envelope that smelled of jasmine. "To Elizabeth Harper. From Denise Bartoni." He breathed heavily through his nostrils and opened the letter without the aid of his letter opener.

*Dear Liz,* wrote Denise. *How are you feeling, m'dear? Your last letter just seemed so sad. I can't even imagine being in your situation. I hope Nick is still being supportive. If he's not... Well, let's just hope that he is. Please always know that I am a phone call away and will hop on any plane at any time if you say the word. I will be in town visiting my mother in two weeks. I would love to have dinner with you, if you feel up to it. Take care and try to smile a little. Your "partner in crime," Denise.*

Nicholas read the letter only once before calmly placing it back in its envelope and walking down the hall to Elizabeth's room. He knocked twice on the door before opening. Elizabeth was curled up on a blue plaid love seat. Her eyes were open, but the room was dark. He walked across the plush white carpet and sat on the bed parallel to the love seat. He said nothing for a moment before extending the letter towards her.

"Here. It's from 'your partner in crime.'"

Elizabeth didn't react. "What does it say?"

He retracted his outstretched hand and placed the letter besides him. "Oh, the usual. 'How are you? Kiss-kiss, call me.'" He rolled his eyes. "And, of course, 'Is Nick still a caveman?' She always has to slide in her little comments about me."

Elizabeth sat up and looked him in the eye. "I'd say she does."

Nicholas grimaced. "She's full of shit."

"At this point, her word is more valuable than yours."

"*At this point*?" Nicholas began. "Seems like her word, and her mother's word, has always been more important than mine."

Elizabeth shrugged. "Maybe they always were."

"You won't even listen to me so how can I even begin to compete?"

She tilted her head. "That's your problem -- you think it's a competition."

Nicholas pursed his lips. "Your faith in their word over mine tells me it's right to think of it as a competition. They don't even know me, Liz. You do."

She shook her head. "I thought I did."

"You do."

Elizabeth looked towards the shaded window. "Then explain Laurel."

Nicholas felt his body stiffen. "Nothing happened, Liz. I never touched her. This... *friend* of yours tells tales out of school and doesn't even come close to talking about the right characters."

Elizabeth's features were unmoved. "Denise wouldn't lie."

"Oh, and I would? I'm treated like a fugitive in my own house and am forced to apologize for something that never even happened. Liz, I love you -- you *know* what that means to me."

She shivered. "All I know is that I got pregnant with a child you didn't want, and you started staying late at the office."

"The baby had nothing to do with it."

She laughed. "No, I'm sure Laurel had at least partial responsibility."

He shook his head and stood up. "Believe what you want." He left the room, closing the door behind him.

He went down the hallway and headed upstairs to the master bedroom. It was the most spacious and extravagant room in the house with a king-sized waterbed and a skylight in the ceiling. He flopped on the bed and bobbed up and down as it settled from the impact. Staring at the skylight, he watched the rain pound the glass and tried to remember what the rays of sunshine looked like through the window. He rolled his head to the side and let his sights linger on a photograph taken of Elizabeth and himself moments after their engagement. He barely recognized the smiling faces, the happy eyes.

*"I'm late, Nick," she'd said so quietly, seated across the kitchen table from him.*

*"For what, Liz? The opera?" he'd said, spooning up a mouthful of Cheerios.*

*"No." She'd looked so young.*

*"For the first day of school?" He'd crunched his cereal.*

*"No! Be serious, please." She'd looked so tired.*

*"I'm as serious as a leprosy colony." He'd winked.*

*"Nick!" She'd looked so scared.*

*"I'm sorry, Liz. Say what you need to say." He'd smiled.*

*"I'm pregnant. We're pregnant." She'd reached across the table.*

His smile had frozen on his face. Her announcement, just weeks after their engagement, went against the grain of all of their plans. Nicholas could still feel the terror build in his stomach hearing the words. *We're pregnant.* He could still see her eyes, as dislocated and hopeful as he'd ever seen any human's eyes. He had wanted to take her in his arms and say it would be all right -- they'd make it all right. But instead, he'd excused himself from the table.

As time went by, the idea of fatherhood became more comfortable for him, but like a glass slipper smashing against the pavement, the foundation of their relationship was already cracked. He became a workhorse, logging hours like a rookie lawyer trying to impress the partners, even though he had no one to impress at Barnes Realty. His uncle was his boss, which spelled job security.

He had no one to impress, that is, except for Laurel Derrikson.

Laurel had started working at Barnes Realty while Nicholas was home painting his house. She was in her mid-thirties, slightly older than himself, and unattached. She was attractive with a slender figure and short red hair. Her smile was dubious and teasing, her eyes always shone with the excitement of the unexpected. She wore short but professional looking skirts, button-down shirts, and a pair of tennis shoes with short socks. Easily classified as a flirt, she brought an air of juvenile fun to the office, and to the company softball team, and Nicholas liked being around her. Everyone liked being around her. She made it easy to be her friend.

*"Nicky, you're a man of principle, right?" Laurel had said one afternoon.*

*"I always thought I was the delinquent student in the last row, but OK," he'd replied with a grin.*

*She'd grinned back and sat on the edge of his desk. "The word around the water cooler is that your fiancé is having a baby. And I was wondering if it was immoral for me to be insanely jealous."*

*Nicholas had raised his eyes in surprise. "Why jealous?"*

*She'd leaned back on his desk. "Because that means you are close to having it all. And I'm so happy for you, it makes me sad because I'm nowhere near as complete as you are. You're a lucky, lucky son of a bitch. Congratulations."*

*He'd smiled. "Thanks. Even though things kind of happened out of order."*

*She'd winked. "There's nothing like a shotgun wedding, Nicky."*

*He'd shook his head. "No one has to put a gun to my head for me to marry Liz. I love her. And I would be marrying her even without this baby."*

*Laurel had brushed her hand across his face before swinging her legs off his desk and walking out of his office. "The first wrinkle in your perfect life may be a blessing in disguise, Nicky," she'd called.*

Nicholas had watched her leave, had fixed his eyes on a noticeable crease in her skirt, and tried to imagine what sort of ironing board could be used to smother the wrinkles in life. He wondered if anyone should even bother to try.

One afternoon when Elizabeth was three months pregnant, Nicholas came home particularly late from the office and found his fiancé lying across the bed asleep. He had smiled and leaned to kiss her, but before he did, he detected the scent of jasmine mixed with orange peels as his eye caught a letter lying on his pillow. It was from Elizabeth's oldest friend Denise. Without even thinking, he picked the letter up and began to read.

*Dear Liz,* wrote Denise. *Is everything OK with you and Nick? I spoke to my mother, and she was concerned about you and your relationship. Honestly, I share her concern! Mother said she ran into Nick's uncle, and he boasted about Nick and the new woman at the office flirting and going for "coffee breaks" together -- a regular office romance. I know you said he's taking the news of your pregnancy hard, but I thought things were getting better? I hate to tell tales out of school, but since this information came from Nick's uncle, who seems to see your fiancé more these days than you, it must be true. Liz, I'm so sorry. Please call me so we can talk. Your "partner in crime," Denise.*

Denise. Elizabeth's oldest friend whom he'd never even met in person.

Denise. That volatile, lying bitch.

He read the letter only once. Once was enough to elevate his blood pressure to the point that the vein in his forehead began to throb. His eyes burned, and he fought the urge to damage her property by shredding the letter. But it belonged to his Elizabeth, and she hadn't shredded it. He turned quickly to look at her.

Sleeping. In their bed.

Doubting him.

He began to pace with the letter clutched in his fist. He wanted to scream. He wanted to shake her awake and make her believe him over Denise. Finally, he hovered over her and brushed his hand over her cheek.

"Liz..." he murmured.

She stirred slightly and blinked awake. "Nick... When did you get home?"

He didn't answer. Instead, he planted his feet and extended the letter towards her.

Her face twitched as she sat up. "Did you read it?"

He continued to extend his hand towards her. "Did you believe it, Liz?"

She bit her lip. "I had a dream a week ago that I was standing on a tight rope that was extended between two skyscrapers. I was crossing it and almost made it safely to the other side when all of the sudden I lost my balance and fell – plummeted -- to the ground. I woke up, and I felt sick to my stomach because I knew that I had lost my balance, I really had." She looked him in the eye. "Because I lost you the moment I told you about the baby."

He remained motionless, the letter still outstretched. "Did you *believe it*, Liz?"

"When I woke up from that dream, Nick, I looked for you to tell you about it and have you tell me it would be OK. But you weren't around. And so I sat and thought about the dream by myself, and as I thought about it, I realized that in the dream I hadn't lost my balance totally unconsciously. I dared myself to fall. I dared myself to fall off the tightrope and dive into the traffic. And I remember getting closer and closer to the ground and half-wondering how it was physically possible that the cars rushing around beneath me were getting taller." She swallowed and diverted her eyes. "The farther away I got from the tightrope -- the closer I got to the ground -- the more I realized that this baby was destroying us."

"Damn it, Liz. Did you believe it?"

A single tear eked out of the corner of her eye and slid down her cheek. "I had an abortion three days ago -- while you were with your uncle and Laurel at the conference in Cleveland. I went by myself." She paused and brushed the tear out of her eye. "When I got home, I called my mother and told her I miscarried."

Nicholas felt his knees grow weak. He glanced down at the letter. "Oh god..."

She looked him in the eye. "I got that letter a week ago, Nick, and Denise never lies."

He sank to the ground. "Oh god..."

"I didn't want you to marry me because of the baby, not if you'd found someone else. I thought it would be easier for you if I just lost the baby. Got rid of it."

"Our baby..."

"I thought that was best," she said.

"Liz... Elizabeth. We should have talked about this..."

He looked up and saw she was crying. "I had enough proof."

"What?"

"I went by the office on my lunch break, and I saw you... In your office... She was sitting on your desk."

"Whatever you think you saw... Liz, you didn't see it!"

"Oh, Nick. I know what I saw." Elizabeth got up and walked across the room. She stood at the dresser for a moment and then turned around with her engagement ring extended towards him. "I suppose you can have this back."

*"Liz, you're the only woman I've ever loved. Will you marry me?"*

*"You're the only man I've ever trusted. Of course I'll marry you."*

He gritted his teeth. "You *suppose*? Goddamn it, Liz! You are not the only person in this relationship."

She cupped the ring in her hand. "Denise wouldn't lie. There was something about you that made me let my guard down -- I thought I could trust you. That was my fault." She paused. "I'm going to go sleep in the guest room."

She left the room, and he was alone with the shards of his broken dream. And now, a few days later, he could do nothing but stare at the skylight and curse the rain. He sat up and rubbed his hands over his eyes and wondered what sort of mortar would bind them back together. Moments later, he got up and walked calmly back down to Elizabeth's room. Without knocking, he entered and stared into the darkness.

The room was empty.

Curiously, he stared up and down the hallway until he detected some movement in the kitchen.

"Elizabeth?" he asked.

"I'm drinking your coffee."

He leaned casually against the doorframe and sighed as he watched her stir her in some milk. "I know this makes no sense, but I wish I was a girl, Liz. I really do."

She eyed him curiously. "What?"

He moved towards her and sat across the table. "I wish I was a girl so that you could believe me. I haven't slept since you told me... Because I keep playing this nightmare over and over in my already overcrowded brain, and it's all a bunch of static. Cobwebs. I should sell the rights to Hollywood and let them root through there and find some sort of truth from all of this. But what it boils down to is... I wish I was a girl. You don't believe a man will tell the truth? I guess your past experiences warrants that opinion. My uncle? He lied. As much as I hate to admit it, Denise and her mother told the truth -- my uncle's truth. But you have to know, whether you believe me or not, that I didn't cheat on you, and I love you, and I loved that child. I don't know how to make you believe me." He got up from the table and headed towards the front door.

She remained motionless. "Part of me wishes you were a girl. So I could trust you. Not being able to trust you is the worst feeling in the world, Nick."

His chin tapped down against his chest. "No, that's not the worst feeling," he said. "Losing a child is."

Nicholas put his coat back on and left the house in silence. He headed back to the corner of Rooster and Lemmings, went past the bus stop and the cemetery, and continued past Johnson to Cavalry Street. He entered the Cammot Inn and headed to the front desk.

"Hello there, cousin Nicky! It's a soggy one, ain't it?" the woman behind the counter asked. "Oh, you'll never believe who checked in this evening..."

He offered a stiff smile. "I don't feel much like small talk tonight, Meg. I need a room. At least for one night," he said.

Meg eyed him and handed him a key. "Everything OK?"

He smiled thickly. "Nothing is OK," he said. He headed over to the wall and pushed the button. Moments later, he was swallowed up by the elevator and ushered up to his temporary home.

Oh, Maria

*You got a piece of me*
*but it's just a little piece of me*
*        "Have You Seen Me Lately?"*

      She sat on the floor in the hallway outside her hotel room with her notebook lying beside her, her chin rested thoughtfully on her bent knees.  Hearing the elevator ping down the hall, she felt herself jolt.  She glanced at the man who emerged and eyed him curiously.  He looked so tired, almost sickly.  Her eyes followed his slow, solemn retreat into his room.

      "He looks almost as lonely as me..." she murmured.

      She glanced down at her notebook and felt a tremor pass through her body as she read the poem, written well over a year ago.

*Guitar Lessons*

*Pick it up -*
*        a piece of wood*
*        hollowed out*
*        by wisdom and laughter*
*        strung through with banded*
*        wire that will*
*        callous your fingers*
*        if you love it enough*
*And hold it close*
*        to you and feel*
*        its cool smoothness against*
*        palms and let your fingers*
*        trace slowly over the surface*
*        and learn its shyness, allow it*
*        to reflect your own*

*Then wake it*
*        by tip-toeing*
*        finger breaths over*
*        the steel banded strings*
*        and hear it sing to you,*
*        even in chaos*
*        and let it echo until*

> *its last vibration fades*
> *Now cherish it -*
> *and explore the harmonies*
> *of your fingers and strings*
> *let your breaths become*
> *sealed and secretive*
> *and washed together,*
> *dashed and spotted,*
> *in a mythical cauldron of spirit*
> *Promise never to put it down.*

She'd scribbled it on the page in blue glitter pen and ignored it until now. She couldn't ignore anything anymore. Standing up, she brushed herself off and considered going to meet the lonely stranger, but she resigned herself to her fate behind her own sullen door.

Turning the knob and entering, she closed the door softly behind her with an excuse-me click. She walked fluidly, almost floating, her bare feet seeming to resist gravity. She moved to the window and closed the shade, banishing the streetlights from the room. Her body was silhouetted against the white curtain, her hand lightly tugging the fabric. She sighed audibly and turned her head. Uncertainly, she stepped towards the bed. Her slip-like white nightgown clung to her body as she sat down and reached her hand towards the pillow.

He closed his eyes as she placed her hand first at the end of his nose and then on his cheek. Her fingers were cool, slightly clammy. He wished she hadn't closed the curtains. He hated the darkness.

"Wake up, Gabe," she said. Her voice was loud in the still room.

"I am awake." He rolled to face away from her.

"How's your head?"

He sat up and stared at her coolly as he leaned over and switched on the lamp beside the bed.

"It's still attached, doctor. Thanks for asking."

She blinked. "You've just been sleeping for so long..."

Gabe stared at the wall. "This place is a real dump."

"I know it's not the Plaza, but it was the closest place off the interstate. And I know how car sick you get when you have a migraine." Maria placed her hand flat on the bed beside his.

He folded his arms against his chest. "We should have kept going. Now we're stuck here in Rinky Dink, Iowa..."

"Ohio, Gabe."

He glared at her. "What's the difference? Ohio, Iowa, Nebraska... Should be one damn state."

Maria stared at the floor. "They're different enough."

He sighed. "Never mind."

Swinging his legs over the side of the bed, he pulled the rumpled t-shirt from the floor over his head and slipped his feet into a pair of tennis shoes. Without looking at her, he headed towards the door.

"The bar is open," Maria said to his back.

With a sardonic look on his face, he rested his hand on the doorknob. "I'm going to go get some ice, Ria. My head is still pounding... And then we're leaving."

"I'll get the ice," Maria said tiredly.

He shook her off. "Just call and get the car out front, OK?"

He opened the door and headed out into the hallway. The carpeting was new and felt cushy under the broken soles of his worn-in tennis shoes. The walls also appeared to be freshly painted. Every breath he drew was filled with the clean, renewed sense of life installed in the old building.

"Maybe I need a fresh coat of paint in the land of cows and corn, too." He smirked.

He headed around the corner and came face-to-face with a door labeled "Ice and Snacks." Looking at his ice bucketless hands, he grinned to himself and backtracked towards the elevator.

"Ice my ass," he said.

Pushing the button, he stood and waited for the ping to alert the elevator's arrival. He stepped inside and hit the first floor button. Once in the lobby, he turned to the left and saw that Maria indeed was right -- the bar was open. He smiled again and headed into the fairly bright dining area. There were only a few people scattered around the room. A young brunette with a maroon vest and black pants hurried over to him.

"Dining room or bar?" she asked.

He leaned casually against a nearby table. "Which section is yours, honey? I'll sit there."

The brunette -- whose nametag read *Stacey* -- looked up in surprise. "But I..." Suddenly her face contorted. "You're... You're... Are you?"

"The bar is fine, honey," he said, patting her arm.

"Gabe Miller!" she said.

He nodded. "And I'm a thirsty bastard."

"The bar it is, then, Mr. Miller." Stacey ushered him through the back of the restaurant and into the more dimly lit bar.

"It's Gabe, really," he said.

"Right. Gabe. Well, sir, enjoy your stay -- your drink. I mean..."

He chuckled. "I will, Stacey. Thank you for your hospitality."

He sat down on a barstool and ordered a scotch and soda. A muted television hung on the wall and was playing a re-run of *The Real World* on MTV. The bartender, an older, gray-haired man with deep wrinkles and a mistrustful look in his eye, set the drink before him and went back to drying a stack of shot glasses.

"Iron in your room doesn't work?" he asked, scanning Gabe's disheveled appearance.

"I couldn't say," he said.

The bartender grunted and narrowed his eyes. His hands slowed their task of drying the glasses as he examined this new, wrinkled patron.

"You that rock star?" he asked after a slight pause.

Gabe sipped his drink to cover his smile. "Yeah."

The bartender grunted and set down his towel. "Say, didn't you just get out of rehab or something?" He leaned the heels of his palms on the bar.

Gabe stared him in the eye, ignored his headache, and gulped his drink. "I'll take another one."

The bartender shook his head and snatched the glass off the bar. "Sure thing, *rock star*."

Gabe took his refill and moved to a small table near the jukebox. Before sitting down, he drew a few coins out of his pocket and slipped them into the machine. Elvis

Presely's "Hound Dog" swam through the air. Leaning back in his chair, he sipped his drink and stared at his own hairy knuckles.

"Uh, I don't mean to bother you, but would you mind signing something for me?"

He looked up into Stacey's anxious eyes. "Sure, babe. What is it?"

"Your new CD. It is so great. It's my favorite since your first -- *With Sprinkles*. Especially the song 'Turn Over Moon.' Those lyrics just kill me! *'Turn over moon and bare your soul tonight--*"

*"--so neither one of us has to be alone or afraid of the sun's rejection. Burn with me, and we'll fuse together in our own plated-gold universe of love and eternity."* He reached over and touched her hand.

Stacey's smile shook. "Yeah. That song just means so much to me."

He took the CD case and examined his own unrecognizable picture embossed on the cover. "You and me both," he said.

After a brief moment's thought, he took the black marker she'd provided and scrawled, *"To Stacey. Thanks for calling me 'sir.' Good luck turning over the moon."* After signing his name, he handed it back to her and watched her face as she read his comment. She grinned, her knuckles turning white from grasping the plastic case.

"Wow, this is... Wow. Thank you," she said.

"No problem," he said.

"I'll go ask Lou if he'll put the CD on," she said, turning toward the bartender.

He caught her retreating fingers softly within his own. "Nah, don't. I don't think he's much of a fan. Besides, I get sick of hearing myself all of the time. Why don't you sit down and have a drink with me instead?" Gabe pushed the chair next to him out with his foot.

Stacey looked anxiously back at Lou. "Yeah, I can take a break."

Gabe's cool smile slid from the girl to the bartender. "Say, Lou. Can we get a little something over here?"

"It's a public place, rock star. Get a room," Lou said, his wrinkles sagging.

Gabe winked at Stacey. "Maybe later," he said.

*     *     *

Maria lay motionless on the bed and stared at the clock. She had considered getting up numerous times, considered getting dressed, considered calling the car to be ready out front. But the clock told her she was right to lie silently, right to ignore his request. The red numbers almost laughed at her. *"What a fool,"* they scoffed. *"This broad thought he'd come back."*

He'd been gone for much longer than his two hours and fifteen minute trip to the ice machine.

Maria sighed and turned her head away from the clock. His acoustic guitar lay in its case flat on the floor near the wall. It was the only thing he'd brought in with him, besides Maria and her own bag. They hadn't been planning on staying overnight; they hadn't even planned on stopping.

They never planned on stopping but plans change.

Maria stared at the guitar case and willed it to open, willed the guitar to suspend itself in thin air and sing to her, like it used to at the Clickwell Coffee House on Amir Street in Gabe's hometown. She longed to hear the painful twinges of the strings, the strummed vibration of emotion, the brush of his callused fingers. She longed to hear its quiet rhythm, its unsuspecting genius.

She closed her eyes and saw Gabe as she had seen him for the first time, on the stool his brother built for him, with his head bent down, his shaggy blond hair shadowing his face, his dark eyes hidden as his fingers did all the talking. She could still feel her breath catch as she walked in the coffee shop; she could still feel the snow melt from her hat and trickle down her neck as she stood motionless in the door. She could still see the slow half-moon rise of his face as he finished playing the last chord of a song he'd just improvised and nod in appreciation at the spattering of applause. She could still see his eyes, glittering and deep, meeting her own, the gaze breaking only when her cousin pulled her away from the door and over to a table.

In the depth of that bitterly cold December night, Maria felt the renewal of spring in her bones.

He played a long set that night, sometimes quiet ballads, sometimes covers of popular rock tunes. Maria never took her eyes off of him. She was intrigued by this character, this artist with an unkempt appearance, sloppily dressed, slouched on a stool, strumming away as a backdrop to coffee house clatter.

"I wish he would sing something," she said to her cousin Melissa.

"Oh, Gabe has a fabulous voice, Maria. He does these amazing covers of Beatles songs," Melissa said, stirring her cappuccino.

"How do you know?" Maria tore her eyes away from the artist -- now with a name, *Gabe* -- and fixed them on her cousin.

"He went to my high school, graduated a year or two ahead of me. He dressed up like a mop top and did a few tunes in this lame talent show we had. That was the year my friend Kimmi Forrest and I decided to do that puppet show. Mom's shown you the video... What a disaster!" Melissa said with a laugh.

Maria sipped the last of her drink. "I'm going to go get a refill. Want anything?"

Melissa shook her head. "Nah, I'm good."

Maria got up and wove her way through the crowd to order another drink. Leaning against the counter, waiting for her mocha, she became acutely aware of a change in the room: it was far from silent, but the chatter stood nakedly, without accompaniment. Her green eyes swiveled to the stool; it was empty.

"Just had to take a break to ice my fingers," a quiet voice said beside her.

She turned her head towards the voice. It was Gabe, his hands clutching towels full of ice cubes. "Oh, right," she said feebly. "Sure, a break."

He smiled, his almost-too-thin lips parting to reveal a gap between his two front teeth. "I'm Gabe," he said, setting down the towels and extending a slightly chapped hand. "Gabe Miller. I'm the sideshow."

Maria laughed. "Hardly a sideshow. You really play well," she said, lightly grasping his clammy hands.

"Yeah, I mean, thanks. It's what I love to do," he said with a shrug.

"I'm Maria Kain, by the way," she said.

"Maria. Pretty name," he said, squeezing her fingers slightly between his own before releasing them.

"Skim double mocha latte with sprinkles!" a voice called from behind them as the drink was slapped on the counter.

"That's me," she said.

"With sprinkles." Gabe nodded. "Yeah, I guess my break's about over."

"Well, it was nice to meet you," she said.

"Same to you. Maybe I'll see you around?"

"Maybe," she said. "I'm just in town for the holidays, visiting my aunt and my cousin."

He followed her gaze back over to Melissa. "I know her. I think we went to the same high school." He smiled. "Well, it's a small town."

Maria smiled back and turned to walk away. Pausing, she glanced back at him; he hadn't moved. "Do you know any Beatles songs?" she asked.

"Every good guitar player does," he said.

"Oh," she said and headed back to her table.

"So was he just as dreamy up close as you hoped?" Melissa teased as Maria sat back down.

Maria laughed. "Oh, dreamier."

She watched him make his way back to the stool and pick the guitar up. He drew in a deep breath and began to play. Maria's breath caught in her throat as she heard him begin to sing.

"*Blackbird singing in the dead of night. Take these broken wings and learn to fly. All your life, you were only waiting for this moment to arise...*"

His voice was quiet at first and then steadily grew louder and louder; the coffee shop was silent by the time his fingers caressed the last chord. Looking up from his guitar, Gabe looked back at Maria and winked.

Maria blinked and shook herself from her daydream. Lying on the hotel bed, she was glad the guitar had stayed in its case, glad that it had resisted magic. So much had changed in the six years since she and Gabe had met at the Clickwell Coffee House on Amir Street. Six years of moving with him from moldy apartment to moldy apartment, motel to motel, city to city, coffee house to bar to small stage to big stage and what did she have to show for it? An absentee lover with no ring on her finger, no child to cling to, no home of her own. She detested her loyalty, detested her commitment, detested her love. She was as much addicted to the scent of him, the taste of him, as he was to cocaine and booze. Every time she said she was through with him, she'd fall off the wagon. They'd fall together from sobriety to numbness. Always together, though, that much was certain. They always fell together.

Rolling over and starring wide-eyed at the ceiling, she ignored the blurred red numbers in her peripheral vision and waited to hear the click of the doorknob.

*　　*　　*

Gabe threw his head back and downed another shot of bourbon. Stacey, giggling, sipped her beer as he bounced her on his knee.

"Just like daddy used to do, eh?" he asked, his bleary eyes rolling towards her.

Stacey hiccuped.

"That's right, baby. I'll take good care of you, just like I was your daddy."

"I'm a big girl, though, daddy," she giggled.

"Just because you're all grown up don't mean you don't need daddy to tuck you in at night," he said with a slight belch.

Stacey put her beer down and semi-rolled off of his lap onto the floor. "Oh!" she said with a soft thud. Laying her head on his knees, she gurgled, "Why don't you sing me a lullaby first."

"Sure, baby. What lullaby would you like to hear?" He patted her on the head.

"Hmm..." she murmured. "Oh, I know. The Beatles one -- the one Ringo sings on the *White Album*. You know, the one that goes 'Now goodnight, something something, sleep tight, something.'" Stacey faded off into a blaze of giggles.

Gabe felt the dull ache in his head start to intensify. "I don't know any Beatles songs," he said, putting his hands on the table.

"Sure you do. You have that cover of 'Blackbird' on that one CD..." Stacey leaned against the chair at the table behind them.

"Yeah, well, I'm not giving a free concert." His eyes darkened like frozen storm clouds.

"What's the matter, Gabe?" Stacey said, her head rolling to the side.

He clenched his jaw. "Listen, baby, it's been fun, but I've gotta mosey along -- gotta keep adding interesting tales to my *Behind the Music* special..."

"Oh, when's that coming out? You tell E! they can interview me..."

"E! does the *True Hollywood Story*, you twit!" Lou called from the bar.

Stacey exploded in giggles. "Oh yeah..."

Gabe ran his hands through his hair and rested his palm on his forehead; he knew he was going to have an awful hangover.

"Whatsamatter, rock star? Need another?" Lou taunted him.

Gabe got up and dragged Stacey to her feet. "Where do you live?" he asked, ignoring the bartender.

She stared at him blankly. "Somewhere..."

Gabe looked from her to Lou. "Do you know where she lives?"

"Why, you wanna go meet her parents and see if they'll let you adopt her, daddy?" he asked.

"Seriously, Lou. She's wasted. I just want to make sure..."

"You just want to make sure your name isn't all over this. Well, rock star, this is a small town," Lou said.

"I just want to see that she gets home OK. That's it," Gabe said as Stacey leaned against him.

Lou's eyes softened a little. "Sure, rock star. I'll make sure she gets home OK."

Gabe nodded and propped Stacey up in front of him. "It's been a blast, baby," he said, plastering one last trademark rock star smile across his face.

She grinned. "I can't believe you're fucking Gabe-goddamn-Miller."

He blinked, narrowing his eyes. "Me neither," he said. Kissing her on the forehead, he helped her over to the bar and onto a stool. "I really appreciate this, Lou," he said.

"No problem, rock star. Anything for the rich and famous," he replied.

Gabe drew a crumpled hundred dollar bill from the pocket of his jeans and threw it on the bar. "Thanks," he said.

The lobby was quiet at one a.m. Staggering to the elevator, he pushed the button and fingered the spot on the nape of his neck where he knew he'd have a hickey. He leaned his head against the wall and wondered if maybe Maria had just left him this time. He wondered if she'd gotten the balls to walk out on him, to swat him from her life, to blot him off her personal canvas. Everyday he gave her a new reason to surrender her love for him, and everyday she forgave him. The emptiness he meant to displace with alcohol built steadily in his system as he waited for the elevator to ping.

When the elevator finally arrived, he climbed on board and rode to his stop. Getting off, he felt his sarcastic smile return as he came face to face with the door labeled "Ice and Snacks." Pleased with himself for considering irony, he went in the room and hit the button on the ice machine; a shower of frozen bullets fell out. He picked one cube up and crunched on it. He picked up another and let it slip through his hands. Watching it fall to the floor, he thought about the ice that speckled Maria the first time he saw her. He thought about how cold it was that day and how, after seeing her, he had forgotten what "cold" was. He picked up another ice cube and chucked it at the Coke machine. Rubbing his numbed fingers over his lips, his bare neck, he felt ashamed for the first time in six years.

He turned and stalked out of the "Ice and Snacks" room and moved stealthily towards his own. He stared at the simple brown door and struggled to detect life inside the room. The door merely shrugged. Breathing deeply, he slid his key in the lock and *click!*

She hadn't moved a muscle. Her eyes were frozen open, staring intently at the ceiling. He stood in the doorway for a moment before moving into the room.

"Ria? You awake?" he whispered.

She said nothing.

He went into the bathroom and splashed water on his face. Looking at his tired reflection, his bloodshot eyes, his graying skin, he wondered if he was, indeed, the oldest twenty-seven-year-old in the world. Disgusted, he flipped off the bathroom light without drying his face.

She was sitting up when he returned, her knees clenched tightly to her chest, her fingers bound around the front. She didn't look at him as she spoke. "I called Denny awhile ago and told him you were staying here tonight. He said everything's set in Cleveland. He said he'd see you tomorrow."

Gabe stood stoically near the bed. "He'd see me tomorrow. Me."

Maria closed her eyes. "You," she said.

"Where are you going to be? Parking the car?" he asked.

Her eyes flashed open. "You would say that," she said.

Gabe looked away. "Damn it... I'm sorry, Ria, I am. I don't know why I say such stupid... I mean..."

"Oh, Gabe, I *know* what you mean. You aren't fooling anyone in this room. So was she pretty?" she asked, her eyes narrowed.

Gabe swallowed. "Yeah, she was pretty."

Maria nodded. "Uh huh. Did you have sex with her?"

"No," he mumbled.

"No? Well, you must not have had your game face on tonight, honey." She laughed. "I don't even know why you'd care if I left."

He looked at her and saw a tear creep down her face. "Oh, Ria. You're not the one leaving. I left you long ago."

Maria covered her face with her hands. "I know."

He moved over and sat beside her on the bed. "Have you seen me lately?" he asked quietly. "Have you seen me at all?"

She shook her head, more from sadness than in response. "Not for years, Gabe."

His body sagged under the truth of her response. "What happened?"

She looked at him. "You're hibernating. You're sleeping. Do you know how I know? Because when you do sleep in bed beside me, I watch you. I watch you close your eyes and surrender your demons for those brief moments that you allow yourself to sleep. I love to watch you sleep. I love to watch your eyelids twitch, and I imagine that you're dreaming about me and not the female you picked up in a bar last week. I watch you breath slowly, regularly, in and out, and it's my only happy time of the day. I love to watch you sleep because it's the only time you're vulnerable, the only time you're uninhibited, the only time you're you -- instead of some stupid rock star. I wish you were sleeping all the time, Gabe, because then I could have you back."

He was silent for a moment, looking at her toes, curled under, hiding their pink nail polish. He flopped his head on the pillow next to her. "Do you remember the first time we heard one of my songs on the radio?"

She stretched her legs out in front of her, folding her hands in her lap. "Sure. It was 'Mellow' and we were in the car going to buy paint for that shitty apartment we were had in Brooklyn." She smiled slightly. "I was driving and nearly crashed when it came on."

He laughed. "That was so amazing, Ria. I mean, the almost crashing wasn't, but everything else about that moment was. Remember? We rolled the windows down and cranked the volume all the way up and sang along.... '*Slinking in the door, passing November, sliding up the banister past sleepy December, I climb in bed and wait for rain to fall...*'" His voice faded off.

Maria swallowed hard as a fresh splattering of rain hit the hotel window. "And we went into that hardware store singing, bought our paint, and sang all the way back home..."

He brushed his fingers across her arm. "Green paint, remember? We painted our living room emerald green, like your eyes, so that I always knew you'd be watching after me, even if you weren't there."

"And who'da thunkit? You're the one who's not around," she said.

He lay motionless for a moment before getting up and moving towards his guitar. Taking it from the case, he moved back over and sat beside her on the bed. Strumming quietly, he looked her in the eye and began to sing.

"*If I need to sleep forever just to dream of you, I will. If I need to dream forever just to hear your voice, I will. If I need to hear forever just to catch your breath, I will. If I need to catch forever just to balance the load, I will. If I need to balance forever just to win your love, I will. If I try to win forever, it will only be in my sleep...*"

They were both quiet for a moment after the last chord faded.

"If life could be fixed forever with a song..." Maria said.

He lay his guitar on the floor and took her hands. "I need your green eyes, I need your pale skin, I need those black skies hovering above your head... I need you, Ria." Leaning in close, he kissed her.

She smiled at him. "I need *Gabe*. If you see him, let him know I'm looking for him," she said. Squeezing his hands and kissing him back, briefly on the cheek, she turned off the lamp and surrendered to sleep.

\*     \*     \*

When he woke up the next day, he was alone in the bed. His head, pierced with pain, lolled slowly to the side as his hand stretched out over where she had been sleeping; it was still warm. He sat up and rested his head in his hands.

"Ria?" he moaned. "Can I get some of that aspirin?"

Silence responded.

Getting up and moving towards the closed bathroom door, he rubbed his temples. "Ria? Come on, baby, don't stay mad."

He pushed the bathroom door open and stared into darkness. Confused, he turned around and saw what he had missed before: a note on her pillow. He blinked and took a brave step back over to the bed. Sitting down in the space she had formerly occupied, he picked the tiny sheet of motel notepaper up and stared at her perfect handwriting.

*Dear Gabe,*

*One of my favorite memories of you is that time we rode in the swan boats in Boston. It was for that stupid photo shoot that Denny set up for you, and you insisted that I be included. Remember? We were sitting in one of those boats in the middle of that pond and you were so happy. You turned to me and said, "Ria, I think I may ask you to marry me so we can have a whole lifetime to turn over the moon." And then you just winked and kissed my ring finger. It was the closest thing I ever got to a proposal from you, Gabe, and I just wanted you to know how much it meant to me.*

*But I can't live like this anymore. You say you need me? I say you need much more than me, and I'm tired of being the only one trying to help you. I will always love you -- Gabe Miller, the Sideshow at the Clickwell Coffee House.*

> *Maria*

*p. s. Your driver will pick you up out front at noon.*

Gabe read the note once and crumpled it up. He glanced at the clock and saw it was nearly time. Picking up his guitar, he turned and headed out of the room. He rested his hand on the doorknob and then turned back. Moving quickly back to the bed, he picked the crumbled piece of paper up and shoved it in his pocket.

Once the elevator hit the lobby, he trudged out towards the door. Suddenly hit with a barrage of flashbulbs, he looked up and saw the entire lobby was plastered with reporters.

"Gabe, how did you enjoy your stay at the Cammot Inn?"

"What do you have to say to your fans in Ohio?"

"When will your next album be set for release?"

"Are you adding any tour dates to your schedule?"

"The buzz says you and a certain Hollywood producer have been in contact. What's the story there?"

He walked slowly through the crossfire of questions without looking up. He wondered how they'd found him and thought of Lou, sour Lou. He couldn't help but grin at the craftiness of that old son of a bitch. As his hand was on the door, he caught one last question:

"Where's Maria, Gabe?"

His fist tightened around the door handle. Turning his head, he said, "I haven't seen her lately," and exited out into the bitter cold of early winter.

In Lights

*We all want to be big big stars,*
*but we got different reasons for that*
                    *"Mr. Jones"*

Gavin snorted when he laughed, a genetic trait passed down patrilinealy. Sitting on the curb outside the New Amsterdam Bar on the corner of Likely and Templeton, he made the generations proud as he laughed at his friend Bob, already slightly drunk, as he tripped over his shoelaces.

"Bobby Jones, acrobat extraordinaire," Gavin said through wheezes of breath. "It's a good thing your mama never had hopes of Olympic Gold for you, son."

Bob straightened himself and grinned without a hint of blush. "Damn straight, Gav. My mama thought I'd grow up to be my old man -- Assembly Line Hal. But you gotta admit, I exceeded that expectation."

Gavin lit another cigarette. "Dude, all you do is hang out with me."

Bob plopped his large frame on the cold cement next to his friend and placed a sloppy arm around his shoulders. "But you're going to be someone, Gavin. And I can say I am your friend."

Gavin blinked and looked away. Sighing, he took a long drag on his cigarette and stubbed it out on the ground.

"Gav, you going to sit there all night or are you coming in?"

He turned towards the familiar voice and waved at the short, brown-haired man standing in the doorway of the bar. "Sure, Lee. I was just waiting for Luna."

Bob pulled his massive body up off the curb. "She'll be here. Let's just go in."

Gavin looked from Bob to Lee and then glanced down the empty street. "OK," he said.

The three of them headed into the New Amsterdam and breathed in the unrelenting stench of smoke, sweat, and beer, and grinned. The place was nearly empty; it was early. Gavin moved out ahead of his friends and sat down at their usual table. He propped his feet up on the wooden chair that would later belong to Luna and lit another cigarette. Bob sat down across from him and slapped the tabletop to watch it teeter on its uneven legs. Lee ordered three beers from Cora, the weekday bartender, and set them down in front of his friends. Sitting backwards in a chair, he nodded towards the stage.

"You performing tonight?" he asked Gavin.

Gavin traced his finger around the cool, smooth edge of his beer glass. "Sure. When Luna gets here."

"Did you write a new one for her or something?" Lee asked.

Gavin smiled. "What can I say? She inspires me."

"Man, I tell you. I never thought I'd see the day when Gavin Macey planned his life around a woman. That bitch has been cracking the whip for you since you met," Bob said.

Gavin stared at him. "Don't call my wife a bitch, Bobby. Ever."

Bob held up his hands. "You know I don't mean nothing..."

"Just don't do it," he said.

The three of them sat in silence for a moment. The entire place was almost totally quiet except for the first-in, last-out regulars Sol and Carmen who were sitting at the bar, flirting with Cora. Sol was an old Sicilian who always wore blue plaid pants and a mismatched gray-striped shirt, and Carmen was a local musician who had the bad habit of getting intoxicated and singing old Frank Sinatra tunes to the bartenders, male or female.

Gavin smoked his cigarette and wondered what future patrons of the New Amsterdam Bar were going to say about Bob. *Bobby Jones: once somebody's friend.* The degradation of un-ambition. Gavin leaned back in his chair and watched the door for Luna, remembering how she'd stumbled into the bar one night by accident. An irregular in a place full of regulars. Gavin looked at Bob and thanked God she had gotten lost in his world.

As the bar grew dimmer with the fading sun, it grew louder with the sounds of glasses clinking, people laughing, and music blaring. The New Amsterdam showcased local talent every day of the week, and the performer of the hour was a grunge rock band called Hail Storm this week (they'd been Verbal the week before). Gavin smoked another cigarette and sucked in the atmosphere. He had grown up in this town, in this bar, the hub of all activity. He had learned to play guitar on the very stage were Hail Storm rained. He had learned to love in the corner booth. He had learned about gravity and how drunkenness does not overrule its laws. He had found his destiny in the four walls of the tiny, dirty bar that sat on the corner of Likely and Templeton.

It was nearly ten o'clock before Luna arrived. She brushed through the crowd and over to Gavin's table. When he saw her, he smiled and got up to embrace her tiny frame.

"What's up, Gav?" she asked, her round face pleasant and relaxed.

"Same shit, different day," he murmured into her thick, blond hair.

She playfully slapped his shoulder. "That's where you're wrong," she said. She pulled a magazine out from under her arm and set it on the table.

"What's that, baby?" he asked, leaning over to get a better look.

"It's Gabe Miller, honey," she said, leaning with him.

Gavin's eyes narrowed as he glanced over the picture of the grimacing rock star, clad in blue jeans and a wrinkled white t-shirt. "You wanna tell me why I'm looking at this, Luna?"

She sighed and sat down in her chair. "Read the caption, Gav."

Gavin pressed his hands flat against the table and read, "'Late for his concert in Cleveland, rocker Gabe Miller made in impromptu visit to the Cammot Inn in the small town of Lanely, Ohio.'" He stopped and looked at his wife. "The Cammot Inn?"

Luna smiled. "Yeah. Isn't that something? Just think, if we would have gotten married a month later, we could have met the son of a bitch."

"I wonder if he stayed in our room..." He sat down next to Luna.

"Says in the article that Maria left him," Luna said, pointing to a section further down. "Says she walked out on him -- right before this picture was taken."

"No shit. Maria left Gabe? Wonder if that bitch is still hanging around Lanely. It's only about forty minutes from here," Bob said as he sat down next to Luna.

Luna rolled her eyes. "Doesn't say, Bobby. But you could always go and find out."

Bob grinned. "Damn, girl. You know I'm saving myself for Leila."

"Only your dream girl would be a stripper," Luna said, lighting a cigarette.

"She is not a stripper. She's a dancer," Bob said defensively.

Gavin laughed. "That's like me saying, 'I'm not a bum -- I'm an artist.'"

Bob nodded. "Yeah. It's just like that."

Gavin shook his head. "Bobby, I mean that I am really just a bum."

"Get up on the stage and say that to me, punk," Bob said with a grin.

Luna rubbed Gavin's arm. "That is one thing that Bobby and I agree on, honey. You're not a bum. And you will make it. You'll make people say, 'Gabe who?' as they're standing in line to see you. Hear you. Your name will be up in lights, baby. I know it."

Gavin brushed his hand across her cheek. "I want to dance with you," he said.

"Sure," Luna said.

"I think I'll get another beer," Bob said, ambling over to the bar.

Gavin and Luna eased their way onto the dance floor and stood completely still in the midst of the sweaty, jumping bodies. Hail Storm thundered through the air as Gavin took Luna's hands and pressed his palms against hers.

"I thought you wanted to dance," she said above the noise.

He smiled. "I do."

"So what are we doing?" she asked, pulling him close to her.

"Dancing," he said with a wink.

She laughed and stepped back. Closing her eyes, Luna's head began to bob with the music and the rhythm seeped through her entire body. Her honey blond hair hung in her face, covering her dark brown eyes, as she began to dance. Gavin followed her lead and before long they were lost, spiraling, in orbits of harsh cords and dense rhythms. They danced until sweat cascaded down their backs, until their mouths were parched, until the music stopped. Only then did they retreat back to their table where Bob had already provided them with drinks, beer for him, gin and tonic for her.

"Hey, where's Lee?" Gavin asked, straddling his chair.

Bob pointed across the bar to the corner booth where Luna and Gavin first kissed. "He's talking to that flamenco dancer instructor from the Y. What's her name?"

"Calia. It's Carmen's daughter," Gavin said.

Luna laughed. "She's probably offering him some tips."

Bob grinned. "Homeboy could use some instruction."

Gavin shook his head. "He'll get more than that from Calia."

Luna chugged her drink. "How would you know?" she asked, leaning across the table.

Bob slid his beer mug in between them. "Let's all be friendly, now..."

Luna raised her eyebrows. "She ever give *you* dancing lessons, Gav?"

Gavin glanced back over at Calia, who was now running her hands through Lee's hair, and grinned sheepishly at his wife. "It's a small town, Luna," he said.

She sat up and folded her arms across her chest. "A smart man would have denied it, Gav."

"My boy is many things but smart ain't one of them," Bob said through a loud burst of laughter.

"Thanks, Bobby," Gavin said.

Bob pounded his hand on his chest. "I'm here for you, bro."

"So is she a good dancer, Gavin?" Luna asked, fluttering her eyelashes.

Gavin scratched his head. "Uh, there's no right answer here, is there?"

Luna shook her head. "But tell me anyway."

Gavin looked back over at Calia. "That's how I met her. Through dancing. Carmen was giving me some guitar lessons, and she showed up in the middle and started up. Bobby was with me, remember?"

Bob nodded. "I think I hit on her."

Gavin waved his hand. "You hit on everyone."

"Yeah, but I want to say that she went home with you that day, Gav," Bob said with a grin.

Gavin buried his head in his hands. "Bobby... Have you met Luna, my *wife*?"

Bob appeared confused. "Uh, yeah, Gav."

Luna laughed. "It's OK, boys. I know that you had a life before me..."

"But life is so much better now that you're in it," Gavin said quickly.

Luna put her hand on his face. "Impeccable timing."

He leaned over and kissed her on the nose. "You dance better than her, anyway."

"Let's not push it too far, honey," she said, patting his cheek.

"Right," Gavin said, leaning back in his chair. He scanned the bar until he locked eyes with Max, the manager. Max nodded at him, and Gavin nodded back. Luna followed her husband's eyes and smiled.

"Your turn?" she asked.

Gavin winked. "Almost," he said. Turning, he caught a glimpse of Carmen and Sol, playing dominoes at the bar. "I'll see you later in bright lights," he said, getting up.

"Gabe Miller who!" Luna yelled.

He leaned over and gave her a quick hug. "You're my Ria, Luna Maria," he said into her hair.

"I wanna give you a kiss for good luck too," Bob said, rolling his eyes.

Gavin waved him off. "Save us all some time and just kiss your own ass, Bobby." Turning, he headed over towards the old men.

"Carmen, hey," he said, leaning in between Carmen and Sol.

"Gavin Macey. Say hello to Sol," Carmen said dryly.

Gavin turned his head and nodded hello to Sol. "Carmen, you interested in a little work tonight?"

"Did you see Calia is over there with your friend Steve..."

"Lee."

"What?"

"Lee. Calia's over there with Lee."

"Who's Lee?"

Gavin clenched his teeth. "My friend."

Carmen chuckled and shook his head. "Always thought that asshole's name was Steve."

"Listen, Carmen. You in or out?"

"Did you clear it with Max?"

Gavin nodded.

"So you wanna play dueling banjoes right in the middle of my game here, son, is that it?"

"That's the idea."

"You ain't no celebrity yet, Gavin."

Sol coughed and scooped the dominoes off the bar and back into their box. "Carmen, leave the boy alone. And get your ass up on that stage."

Carmen nodded once. "Let's go," he said.

Gavin and Carmen climbed the three stairs to the stage and slipped behind the curtain. Drawing a silver key from his back pocket, Gavin unlocked the door to Max's office and the two men went in. Propped against the wall were four guitars and a mandolin. Gavin and Carmen said nothing as they each chose a weapon and left the office.

The two of them felt their way back through the semi-darkness and stood behind the thin, black curtain. The bar was at a high-impact murmur complemented by some hard rock on the jukebox and the sound of glasses hitting tables. Gavin heard Carmen breathing quietly beside him, even over the crowd.

"Now," he said.

The two men pushed their way through the curtain. Each of them pulled a stool along with him and propped it behind the microphone. The patrons of the New Amsterdam didn't pay any attention to them as they set up and sat down. When they were ready, Gavin caught Max's eye. Max signaled for the jukebox to be turned off and whistled sharply.

"Stage, people!" he yelled.

The familiar call from the manager caused heads to swivel towards them, and a few people clapped and cheered when they saw who was about to perform. Gavin caught Bob's eye, and Bob raised his beer glass to him as Luna whistled. Calia and Lee had joined them at the table.

"I'm Gavin Macey, this is Carmen san Rio, and we're going to play a little for you all tonight," he said after a brief pause. "What should we start out with tonight, Carmen?"

"Hell if I know," Carmen said with a wink.

The two of them had sat on that stage countless times, and they always started with the same song: "Mr. Jones." It was the first song Gavin had written after Carmen taught him how to play the guitar. It was recognizable to most of the New Amsterdam regulars, and many of them would sing along. Gavin and Carmen picked up their guitars and began to play.

Gavin's throaty voice lead the bar in song:

"*Mr. Jones and me, hanging out at the New Amsterdam, looking up at the stage and wondering when it will be our turn in the lights. Bright lights. I wanna see my name in fireworks across the sky, across the stage, across the map of our nation. Mr. Jones wants to be famous, too. We sit in the back of the bar and stare at the microphones and wonder if we can use them as light sabers, as weapons of words, and I know that one day we will both be on the stage, singing and laughing, drinking and smoking, and we will have everything we want. Yeah, everything we want. Someday we will learn to play these damn guitars and we can watch the whole world dance at our feet, yeah, dance at our feet. Mr. Jones and me will make it - -we will make it far. Can't you see it now?*"

The crowd whistled and cheered as the last chord faded. Gavin and Carmen smiled and waved at the regulars who had joined in the song. Bob stood up and whistled loudly.

"Only problem with that damn song is that Mr. Jones never learned to play the guitar!" he yelled.

Gavin laughed. "It's OK, Bobby. Everyone, there's Mr. Jones. Tell him he's not a loser."

A few people threw some peanuts off the tables at Bob amidst cheers of, "Jones!" Bob grinned and took a bow. As Bob worked the crowd, Gavin locked eyes with Luna and smiled.

"This next one's for my wife," he said loudly. Luna's face brightened with surprise. He picked up his guitar, never took his eyes off of her, and began to play.

"*I have been searching my whole life for something beautiful. For something beautiful to hold on to, to make mine. Something beautiful to make me whole. I've been searching all my life to find that piece that fits with me, to complement the gray in my portrait, to finish off my dreams.*

"*I was a fool searching for something, for something beautiful. I was a fool, a fool, searching for something I couldn't have.*

*"When I met you, time began and everything from before was nothing but a primer, nothing but a buffer. Time began when our breaths became one, our breaths became one, and we could breathe for days off one lung. When I met you, time started over and nothing that happened before mattered at all. Not at all.*

*"I was a fool searching for something, for something beautiful. I was a fool, a fool, searching for something I couldn't have.*

*"You and I, we swung from the moon, ah, my Luna, my Luna, I love the stark light in your eyes, that light that reflects. You glow from our love, yeah, you glow from our love. You reflect our love while I just swing, just swing, just swing.*

*"I was a fool searching for something, for something beautiful. I was a fool, a fool, searching for something I couldn't have.*

*"We all want something beautiful. We all want something beautiful to make us feel whole, to make us feel whole. But, baby, we don't need something beautiful. Together, we are happy and that's even better than beautiful, even better. Luna, my Luna, I was searching all my life for you.*

*"I was a fool searching for something, for something beautiful. I was a fool, a fool, searching for something -- and it seems that what I've found is you. Just beautiful."*

As he stroked the last chord, an eerie silence filled the New Amsterdam bar. Gavin set his guitar down on the stage and raised his eyebrows towards his wife.

"This is his wife!" Bob yelled as he pointed his thick fingers towards Luna.

The New Amsterdam burst into applause as Luna's face turned a deep shade of red.

"Yeah, folks, she's my wife and if she wasn't already married to me, I'd ask her to marry me again," Gavin said.

The crowd laughed, and then Carmen and Gavin played a few more songs together. Once Carmen got tired, Gavin stayed up on the stage alone and sang original song after original song. Lee and Calia controlled the dance floor while Bob had a beer with Carmen and Sol at the bar. While Gavin played, Luna sat at the table, unmoved and smiling, until her husband called it a night. By then, the bar was mostly empty.

"You know, Gavin, you should really put a demo tape together," Max said as Gavin put his guitar away.

"Oh, I have. It's out there, Max, just waiting for a break."

"Too bad you're stuck in this shittin' little town," he said.

Gavin tucked his arm around Luna and waved good-bye as Lee and Calia strode out the door on the heels of Carmen and Sol. "I'm not stuck, Max. Just living."

With that, Luna, Gavin, and Bob all called goodnight and headed out into the cold, December air. Standing on the corner of Likely and Templeton, Gavin lit Luna's cigarette and leaned against the street sign. Bob stood thoughtfully nearby.

"You know," he began, "as much as I love you, Gav, and I really do love you, I think Max is right."

Gavin raised his eyebrows. "Do you?"

Bob nodded. "You deserve better. I mean, your talent deserves a bigger showcase than the New Amsterdam stage."

"Ah, Bobby. Someday, maybe."

"Soon, Gav," Luna said, poking him in the ribs. "You're gonna be a big star."

Gavin grinned. "I've already got the moon," he said.

"So you have," Luna said, putting out her cigarette. "And it's time for this moon to say goodnight." She turned and smiled at Bob. "'Night, Bobby."

"Yeah, Luna. Goodnight to you. And Gavin -- I'll see you tomorrow?" Bob asked.

"Sure thing, Mr. Jones," Gavin said.

With that, the three of them parted ways, Bob off down Templeton and Luna and Gavin off down Likely under separate shields of streetlights and icicles.

An Accident

*I can't remember all the times I tried*
*to tell myself to hold on to these moments*
 *as they pass*
                    *"A Long December"*


It was nearly two-thirty in the morning before Eddie was able to feel again. He sat in the hallway outside of Jules' room with his head in his hands as his eyes peeled open, dry and weary. He stared at the ugly swirl of pastel lines on the carpet. Slowly, he rubbed his thick hands through his dark, greasy hair and wondered how he had managed to sleep. His legs were stiff and tingling, the muscles in his back were tense and drawn. He could do nothing but open and close his lips, and even then his joints popped.

"Go in and say good-bye, if you want," a voice beside him said.

Without looking up, Eddie moaned. "Can't," he said.

He felt the shadow beside him move away just as swiftly as it had descended, and he fixed his eyes intently on a particular strain of aqua on the floor. He blinked and wondered if the nurses would give him some morphine, feed it to him intravenously, if he asked politely. He wondered how long he could live on numbness.

"Eddie, get your ass in the room."

Eddie's head snapped up at the tenor of the new voice. His own greenish-gold eyes locked with his uncle's wide, black pupils. Eddie froze for a moment, thawed only by the wheezing cough of his aunt in the next room.

"Yes, sir." He forced his legs to bend, forced his body to move.

Step. Forget regrets. Step. Forget the past. Step. Forget laughter. Step. Forget time. Step. Forget family. Step. Forget needles. Step. Forget touching. Step. Forget love. Step. Forget debts. Step. Forget healing. Step. Forget pain. Step. Forget Jules. Step. Forget. Step. It. Step. All. Step.

Eddie walked like a sleepwalker, lumbering and awkward, as he made his way into Jules' hospital room. His aunt Sofia stood by the large window overlooking the terrible neighborhood they lived in. She had a serene smile on her face, her arms folded pleasantly across her front, her body leaning against the cool glass.

"It's snowing," she said without turning around. "And there are people out there enjoying it."

Eddie slouched beside her and stared out at a happy couple kissing under a streetlight. "That's the guy who sings at the New Amsterdam Bar," he said.

"How nice," Aunt Sofia replied.

"Jules calls him 'the next big thing.' He keeps hassling him about letting him be his manager, like he knows anything about being a manager..." His voice faded away.

Eddie turned away from the window and rested his eyes on Jules. His cousin lay quietly in the bed, his arms folded in the same comfortable way across his chest as Sofia's were across hers, his brown eyes mischievously closed, his brown hair matted and plastered against his head. Eddie sat down in the chair beside his bed and reached out an awkward hand to touch him. His fingers brushed Jules' elbow, and Eddie was surprised at how warm the flesh felt. Turning towards his aunt, Eddie opened his mouth to speak but closed it just as quickly when he saw a lone tear creeping down her face.

"It's so nice to see happy people," Aunt Sofia said, brushing the tear away and smiling again. "That lovely couple is building a snowman on their porch."

Eddie bowed his head and folded his hands in his lap. He closed his eyes and saw his aunt smiling even in the darkness.

"I called your mother," his uncle said, suddenly stepping into the room. "She's flying in from California."

Eddie looked up slowly and felt the bones in his neck creak. "Oh."

His uncle frowned and stepped back out into the hallway.

"Never mind him, Eddie. You know how he gets around the holidays," Aunt Sofia said, clutching her arms even tighter against her body.

Eddie clenched his jaw and reached his hand out towards Jules again. Resting his palm on his arm, he swallowed hard and waited for something to happen. A miracle. Jules was famous for his miracles at the horse track, his golden poker face. Eddie needed that same charm to come through now. Something to erase the smell of the hospital from his mind. Something to make Jules wake up. Something to end his solstice depression.

But there wasn't even the beeping of the heart monitor, the whirring of medical voodoo, to delude him.

*"He's dead. At least that's what the doctors said."*

His uncle had delivered the news to him in the hospital cafeteria. He had stood behind his nephew, without touching him, and walked away before another word could be spoken. Eddie couldn't even remember how how'd gotten from that tiny, graffiti-covered table to Jules' room, and he couldn't remember when he had sat down in the plush, fuchsia chair and allowed the coma to take over. Now as he sat in the room, he stared intently at Jules' nostrils, waiting for proof that science was wrong, that medicine was wrong. Waiting for his cousin to wake up. Waiting for something to go right. Eddie closed his eyes.

"Maybe your mother will bring you some of those candies you like," Aunt Sofia said.

Eddie opened his eyes and stared at her. "Maybe." He turned back to Jules' serene face and felt a pang of envy wash over him. "Maybe," he repeated. Standing, he touched his aunt gently on the shoulder before lumbering out of the room. His uncle leaned against the wall outside of the door, his large frame slouching and tired.

"Where do you think you're going?" he asked.

Eddie walked calmly away, feeling his joints becoming more limber with each step. "Home," he said.

"You've got no home, boy," his uncle said. "You've got nothing."

Eddie headed down the hallway until he reached the staircase and ran down the steps three at a time. When he hit the last one, he shoved open the door and walked through the nearly vacant lobby. He paused a moment before heading out through the automatic glass doors and onto the street. Out of habit, he reached into his pocket for his car keys before remembering that his keys were fused into the ignition of the car which was totaled. Shoving his hands deep into his pockets, he wished he had a hat and trudged off down the street. Glancing up, he wondered if his aunt could see him walking away, walking away from the problem like he always did. He hoped she could see him. He hoped she could see that some things didn't change in a split second. That some things never changed.

He walked the three blocks to the Hillside Manor Cafe, open twenty-four hours a day, seven days a week, and made it in just before all of his joints became frozen. A few of the regulars had sprawled themselves out in the smoking section and occupied nearly all of the booths. He sat down at a table in nonsmoking and pulled his pack of Marlboros out. Setting them on the table, he fished for his lighter and flicked it to watch the flame dance. His face remained stoic as he lit the flame over and over, his eyes intently gathering in the particles of light.

"Coffee, Eddie?" asked Betty, one of the late-shift waitresses. She stood beside him and yawned as she automatically filled his cup and walked away before he could reply.

Eddie pulled a cigarette out of the pack and lit it. Instead of smoking it, he set it on its end and watched the tip smolder.

"This is your brain on drugs," he murmured. His eyes were locked on the growing stem of ash.

"Hey, Eddie, smoke that in the smoking section, would ya?" Betty called from the kitchen.

"Sure," he said without moving.

"Ah, Betty, lay off him, OK? No one's sitting up there, anyway," one of the regulars said from behind last week's Sunday paper.

Eddie put his cigarette out in an empty coffee cup and went back to fiddling with his lighter.

"Say, Eddie, where's that asshole cousin of yours?" shouted Jeff, another regular, playing cards in the back booth.

"Oh, he's dead tonight so he won't be in. Why, does he owe you some racetrack money?" Eddie asked, flicking his lighter.

Jeff's jaw dropped. "What did you say?"

Eddie closed his eyes and listened to the quick burn of the flame. "I asked if he owed you money."

Jeff got up and moved slowly towards him. "That's not what I mean, asshole, and you know it. Did you say that Jules is dead?"

Eddie set the lighter down. "Yes."

Jeff sat down next to him. "What the hell happened?"

Eddie spun the lighter around on the smooth tabletop. "There was an accident."

"Shit. Was anyone else hurt?"

Eddie shook his head. "No."

"Jesus, man, I'm sorry," Jeff said. After an awkward moment, he got up and headed back to his own table. "I'm really sorry, Eddie."

Eddie's face remained placid. "If he owed you money, let me know. I'll make sure you get paid."

"Refill, Eddie?" Betty asked, materializing beside him, still yawning.

"No thanks." His eyes lingered on Jeff. "I don't need anything at all."

"Sure thing, honey," she said, walking back into the kitchen.

Eddie rolled his shoulders and felt his muscles yawn, felt his muscles beg for oblivion. He tapped his fingers in a steady rhythm on the table and watched the snow fall.

He sat uninterrupted until the last of the late night regulars ambled out into the blistering wind, and the morning crowd began to filter in. Only then did he sweep his belongings into his pocket, leave his standard three dollars on the table, and merge into the land of the living. Standing on the frozen sidewalk outside the Hillside Manor Cafe, he shoved his hands in his pockets and wondered where he should go. He looked at the people hurrying by him and headed toward the only sense of life he had left.

The half-mile he normally drove to Maya's house seemed an eternity on foot, especially in the cold. Once he stepped up onto the familiar moldy porch with the sunken wooden steps, he felt a rush of heat spread through his body as he breathed in the stench of beer-stained wood and the inexplicable scent of mothballs that always greeted him. He knocked on the screen door and then sat down on the porch step. Drawing his package of cigarettes from his pocket, he lit another and held it between his fingers. Moments later, he heard the door creak open.

"Hi, Eddie," Maya said through the screen. "Let me get my coat, OK?"

Eddie said nothing, his eyes intently following the wispy stream of smoke from his cigarette. Maya soon slipped out of the house, wrapped in a thick winter coat and a large red quilt. Her long brown hair was stringy and fell across her face as she sat down beside him, her wide brown eyes sad and tired.

"Can I bum a smoke?" she said after a slight pause.

He offered her the pack. "Jules is dead."

Her hand rested on his as she reached for a cigarette. "I know."

He searched her face. "Did my aunt call...?"

She shook her head. "It was in the paper this morning. I'm so sorry, Eddie."

Eddie stubbed out his cigarette. "Reduced to a headline, eh?" He laughed. "What did it say?"

Maya shrugged. "Said Jules crashed your car into a tree early last night."

"It said my car?" Eddie asked incredulously.

A brief smile flitted across her face. "No, but I know it was your car. There's no way your uncle would let him drive his."

Eddie reached his hand up to touch her face, and she drew back instinctively. He blinked. "Yeah, it was my car," he said.

Maya shivered. "Anyway, I'm sorry, Eddie."

Eddie looked away. He squinted his eyes as he peered down the empty street full of broken-down houses. "My mom's flying in from California."

"Oh?"

Eddie nodded. "Yeah, she's breaking her own rule never to set foot in Ohio again." He chuckled. "Figures it'd happen in winter, too. She ran away to the warmest, sunniest place she could find because she wanted to suntan-over her problems. And look how Ohio's going to greet her on her less-than-triumphant return -- there's even snow."

Maya held her hand out and caught a few of the fat flakes. "I don't know how anyone could want to escape this," she said with a smile.

He felt the muscles in his face tweak. "I want to escape," he said.

The smile slipped from her face. "I know you do."

He placed his palms flat on the sunken wood behind him and leaned back. "Jules wanted to escape, too, you know. There must be something in our blood that makes us what to get the hell out of here." He laughed. "Or maybe it's just my uncle that makes us all want to leave. It's hard to say."

Maya took one last drag on the cigarette before flicking it onto the sidewalk. "No, it's not." She studied his face. "There's a lot locked away in you, Eddie. And I think your uncle holds the key to most of it."

Eddie shrugged. "Must be why he's a locksmith."

Maya frowned. "The problem is, every time I see you, you've changed the locks, and I can never figure out how to get in."

He stared straight ahead. "Jules always knew how to read me. He always did. He would always say just the right thing, do just the right thing to set me back on track. It's like I was the blind man but Jules was the one who could read the Braille. He could help me even when I didn't know how I needed to be helped." Eddie looked at her. "Now what?"

She smiled. "Well, you're here. That's something."

Eddie laughed. "Yeah, with my ex-girlfriend. That's something."

Maya sighed and stood up, putting the quilt on the top step. "Let's walk," she said.

Eddie nodded. "OK."

They walked in silence down the block amidst the sleeping homes. Without realizing it, he reached over and took her hand, and she let him. Their fingers hung desperately together in a familiar locking grip.

"I have always had trouble with December," Eddie said finally.

She glanced sideways at him. "Yeah, I remember."

"Decembers are just so long and hard to stomach. Look around at all of these cheap Christmas decorations, flashing lights, hokey Santa Clauses, cheap manger scenes... All bullshit. December makes my intestines tie in knots. I mean, the whole fucking month is devoted to the build-up to the 25th. We're forced to listen to Deck the Halls and Silver Bells beginning after Halloween all the way through December just because of one lousy day. Christ," he muttered. "It's sick."

"It's not supposed to be like that, though, Eddie. I mean, it's not like that for everyone," Maya said.

"Well, then the rest of the world can kiss my ass and meet my uncle's fist -- no, better yet, his belt -- and then they can tell me what the hell I have to be happy about.

December really is all about the 25th." He paused and laughed, the staccato vibrations freezing and falling slowly to the ground. "I'm all about the 26th. Hell, Maya, I'm twenty-three years old and the greatest day of my year is the 26th of December because that's when people stop shoving Christmas down my throat. Twenty-three. And I can't think of one Christmas, one December, that I was happy."

Maya sighed. "You're never happy, Eddie. Not any time of year."

Eddie squeezed her hand. "You used to make me happy."

She loosened her grip. "You used to make me miserable."

Eddie looked at the ground. "I'm sorry about that."

"Me too," she said.

"Jules always said I should ease up on you. He always said, 'Eddie, Maya's a good woman. You've gotta respect her.'" Eddie looked at her. "I did respect you. I mean, I do. I'm just not very good at dealing with relationships. They're all so complicated."

"The back of your hand often uncomplicated things for me, Eddie," Maya said quietly.

Eddie felt a chill run down his back, and he let go of her hand. Stuffing his fists into his pockets, he stared straight ahead. "Maya, I don't know how many more ways I can ask for forgiveness."

"I've forgiven you, Eddie. You've cleaned up your life since then -- stopped the drugs, eased up on the drinking... I'm sorry I even brought it up."

"Jesus, so am I," Eddie said.

"It's just that before when you went to touch my face..."

"I know."

Maya shoved her own hands in her pockets. "I'm sorry I brought it up," she repeated.

"Don't apologize. It's good for you, for anyone, to remind me. Jules used to remind me about all of the stupid stuff I'd done all the time, and it was the best thing for me, even though I always hated to hear it. He used to say, 'Eddie, for you life is a bunch of oysters and no pearls.' I guess he was right."

"No, Eddie. Your life can be magnificent if you want it to be. I remember the first time I met you..."

"At the party in Richie Learner's basement..."

"And I saw you looking at me from across the room..."

"You looked so damn beautiful standing under that light..."

"And I knew right then that you were someone special." Maya stopped walking and turned to face him. "Eddie, I knew that first day that I would fall in love with you. And I did."

Eddie looked away. "Until I fucked it up."

Maya paused. "We just weren't made for each other, that's all, Eddie. But we were made to know each other, to be part of each other's lives."

"I wonder if I'm supposed to be part of anyone's life."

Maya studied him. "Why do you say that, Eddie? You've got so much to offer."

"What have I got to offer but an empty shell?" He looked her in the eye. "I was in the car with Jules when it crashed into the tree. He died, and I lived. I didn't even get a damn scratch on me, Maya. Jules, who loved life despite my uncle, died and I lived. When I can't even say the word 'lived' without choking on the sound of it. God messed up. He should have just taken me."

Maya touched his arm. "But He didn't."

Eddie closed his eyes and swore he could hear the scratching of his dry lids as they covered his sandpaper eyes. "No."

Maya smiled. "Maybe you should go and see your mother."

Eddie nodded. "Maybe."

He walked her back to her house and kissed her on top of her head. Waving slightly, he headed back down the road towards town. Stopping at a pay phone, he dialed his uncle's house.

"Hello?" his aunt said.

"Sofia, it's Eddie. Is my mother there?" he asked.

"Oh, she called and said she wasn't going to come after all, dear. Really, I told her not to make a special trip. No need to pull her away from where she's needed."

Eddie's face fell. "She's not coming?"

"Well, no. She said she's really busy with work. But she sends her love."

Eddie bit his lip and choked on the bile building up in his throat at the sound of his aunt's cheery voice. "Sure. OK."

"Will you be home later, Eddie?" Aunt Sofia asked. "Your uncle's at the shop, and it's pretty quiet around here."

"Maybe later," he said as he hung up the phone.

Standing on the street corner, Eddie scanned the modest crowd of people hurrying to finish the last of their holiday shopping and felt a twinge of envy at their happiness. He walked along until he spotted a cab. Getting in, he directed the driver to take him to Blues Field. Once he reached his destination, he got out of the cab and stood in the half-empty parking lot, staring at the empty track. It was one of Jules' favorite places to go: the horse track. Blues Field was closed to outdoor races in the winter, but he knew that the stakes were still high inside the building as people placed bets on their surefire horses racing at tracks in warmer climates. Standing in the parking lot, Eddie wondered if God had placed His bets on him. Looking up at the sky, he knew that Jules had died despite his happiness and wondered if he could live despite his depression. Sucking in a gust of December grime, Eddie trudged towards the building to find out what the stakes were in the house that day.

# If Wishes Were Horses

*Margery's wingspan's all feathers and coke cans,*
*and TV dinners and letters she won't send…*
*       "Another Horsedreamer's Blues"*

Margery sat alone in a fat, cushioned chair near the window looking out over the cluttered parking lot of Blues Field. Her eyes carefully sorted through the maze of cars crusted with salt and petrified by the dust of winter. She saw car doors slam open and close as people, mostly men who looked like her father, hurried towards the building. Her eyes rested for a moment on a young, greasy-haired man with no hat and an unzipped coat who was looking up at the sky. Margery rolled her eyes in disgust.

"God won't help you place your bets." She swung her legs out and stood up.

She narrowed her eyes as she scanned the indoor crowd. Margery longed for the haziness of spring and the re-opening of the outdoor track. She hated the claustrophobia of indoor races being broadcast through electronic tubes. Moving slowly towards the row of big-screen televisions, she shivered and wondered why her cheeks weren't flushed with the same enthusiasm as the rest of the patrons. She stood behind a couch piled with coats and scarves and stared at the backs of the heads of the people who were chanting for their dogs. Margery never cared much for dog racing, though, and moved on down the line.

"You bettin' today, missy?" a voice said behind her.

Margery didn't move as the man who owned the voice placed his hand on her hip. "My horse is racing later," she said.

The man slid around in front of her without removing his hand. "Can I buy you a drink while you wait?"

Her face remained unchanged. "Sure," she said.

The man escorted her towards the club restaurant and pushed her to a seat at the bar. The room was nearly empty except for a few early lunchers and late breakfasters. The man sat down next to her and pulled a cigarette out of his pocket.

"Mind if I smoke?" he asked as he lit the cigarette.

"Yes," Margery said.

The man laughed. "I've seen you around here before, missy," he said as he blew the first drag of smoke through his nose. "You're a pretty smooth operator."

Margery coughed loudly and waved the dark cloud away from her face. "Thanks."

The man leaned back on his barstool and winked at her. "What would you like to drink?"

She turned towards the bartender, who looked too young to serve alcohol, and said, "I'll have a Coke. In a can, please."

The bartender nodded. "And for you sir?"

The man's eyes remained on Margery. "I'll have a martini. Dry."

"Coming right up," he said.

Moments later, the bartender set their drinks in front of them. He offered Margery a glass, but she waved it away. Flipping open the tab, she sipped the sweet, brown liquid and glanced at the clock.

"You could have gotten something else, you know," the man said.

Margery shrugged. "I wanted a Coke."

"What, you don't start drinking real liquid until after lunch?"

Margery took a long sip and stared at the man. "I don't consider alcohol to be 'real liquid.'"

The man snorted. "You're one of those types, are you? Alcohol against your religion?"

Margery's eyes wandered over the sparse crowd. "I'd have to have a religion in order for drinking to be against it."

The man stared at her. "I guess," he said.

"Thanks for the drink," she said, getting up and walking out of the restaurant. The man didn't follow her.

She glanced at the clock again and saw it was nearly time for her race to begin. She headed back into the room with the televisions and stood quietly behind the couch.

"You know Benson jinxed that new filly of his by naming her Sure Thing," said an older, sour looking man sitting on the couch.

"Yeah, but Sure Thing comes from great stock--she was sired by Rose's Thunder Lily and Yankee Doodle Dancer," said the old man sitting beside him.

"It'll take a while to tell, Grandpa," said a younger man standing near the windows. "But I'd bet on Sure Thing. In fact, I did."

The first man waved his grandson off. "Damn fool. Waste of money. This race is going to Tiyuri. I've been tracking that horse for weeks."

"Perfect Dozen's up there, too, though, Dell," the second man said.

Dell grunted. "He might place, but that new jockey doesn't have as good command of him as Martinez did."

Margery listened intently to the conversation with her eyes closed. She thought of the three hundred dollars, the last of her stash, in the hands of the bookie downstairs. Her eyes flew open as the announcer cried, "And they're off!"

The old men and the grandson leapt to their feet with the other patrons while Margery stood behind them. Her eyes were glued to the television screen, glued to the horse in blue. She felt her lungs condense as the horses rounded the final stretch, with Perfect Dozen in first place. She felt her mouth grow dry, her stomach cringe, her nostrils flare in anticipation, in pure exhilaration.

"And it's Tiyuri taking the lead from Perfect Dozen in the last leg of the race! Tiyuri's the winner!" the announcer cried.

Margery drew in a deep breath and smiled. Her knees felt weak, and she leaned against the couch with her palms flat against the cheap fabric. Dell turned to his companions and laughed. "What'd I tell you boys? Old Dell knows who to bet on!"

Margery felt a quiet calm come over her as she headed to collect her winnings. After cashing out, she exited Blues Field and plopped herself down on a bench beside the bus stop. She had no winter coat and shivered despite the extra sweater she pulled over her head. Glancing up at the green-tinted sky, she was half-tempted to forget herself and smile, but the sound of Devon's voice in the back of her head stopped her.

*"Horses are pipe dreams, Margie. One day, you'll wake up and realize you're alone and that you've given your life to gambling. I'm just glad I won't be around to see you fall. Because you'll hit hard, Margie, you really will."*

The sun blinked over her like the red eye of Hal.

She felt the money in her pockets, seven one hundred dollar bills, and her breath began to quicken. She glanced around the parking lot looking for the bus, and she felt the pit in her stomach grow.

"You need a ride?" a voice said beside her.

Her head turned slowly to face the smiling young man who'd bet on Sure Thing.

"No, I'm just waiting for the bus," she said.

"Dell, come on now, boy!" a grumpy voice called from the fogged windows of a new white Cadillac.

"You're Dell, too?" Margery asked, glancing towards the commotion.

"Too?" Dell asked, ignoring the beeping horn of his grandfather's car.

She nodded towards the Cadillac. "I saw you inside."

Dell smiled. "I saw you in there, too. Let us give you a ride."

Margery's eyes traveled to the Cadillac and saw Dell Senior intently rubbing the condensation from the interior of his windshield as he lay on the horn.

"Your grandpa looks like he's in a hurry."

Dell waved her off. "It was his idea, Miss..."

Margery stood up slowly and crossed her arms firmly across her chest. "I'm Margery. Just Margery."

"Well, Just Margery, let us take you where you're going," Dell said, lightly tugging her sleeve. He led her over to the car and opened the back seat door. "After you," he said.

Margery climbed in and slouched on the cold, leather seats. Dell Senior peered at her in the rearview mirror and grunted. Dell Junior walked around the car and climbed in beside Margery.

"Grandpa, Mr. Matthews, this is Just Margery," he said cheerily.

"Just Margery?" Dell Senior repeated. "Were your parents hippies?"

Margery's eyes darted between the Dells, one smiling, the other scowling. "Yes," she said.

Dell Senior narrowed his eyes. "Oh," he said.

"It's nice to meet you, honey," Mr. Matthews said from the front seat without turning around. "Let's go, Dell. Mrs. Matthews is making beef stew for lunch."

Dell Senior pressed his foot on the gas and sped out of the parking lot. "Where are we taking you, Just Margery?" he asked as he turned left, away from the heart of town.

"She's coming with me," Dell Junior said with a wink.

Margery sighed and glanced out the window. "Sure."

"What were you doing at Blues?" Mr. Matthews asked after a moment.

"Betting on the horses." Her breath beat stiffly on the window.

Mr. Matthews turned his head slightly. "Really? And how'd you do?"

"My horse won."

Dell Junior laughed. "You must have bet on Tiyuri, then."

Margery nodded.

Dell Senior slapped the steering wheel. "Ha. The girl's got some brains."

The Cadillac rolled away from the city and into the suburbs, stopping outside a white brick apartment building.

"This is our stop," Dell Junior said with a wink.

"OK," Margery said, resting her hand on the door. "Thanks for the ride."

"Anytime, smartie," Dell Senior grunted.

Dell Junior ran around the car and helped her out. Waving at the retreating car, he laughed. "That old sonovabitch..."

Margery stood stoically beside him. "He knows his horses, though."

Dell nodded absently. "Makes my grandmother insane." He turned and headed towards the building. "Can I interest you in some coffee, Just Margery?"

"Margery," she said.

"What?"

"It's kind of irritating when you call me 'Just Margery.'"

He waved his hands around and leaned against the door. "I'll call you Helen of Troy if it makes you happy."

She remained unmoved by the curb. "Listen... I think I'm going to get going."

Dell frowned. "It's just coffee, Margery."

She sighed and let her eyes linger on the crisp, white exterior of the building. "It's never just coffee," she said, turning and heading down the sidewalk. "But maybe I'll see you at Blues again."

Dell tossed his keys from one hand to the other. "No," he said.

Margery stopped and turned around. "What?"

He began walking towards her. "No. We'll go to your place." He was standing close to her, near enough for his frozen breath to hit her face. "At least let me give you a ride."

Margery frowned. "Fine."

Dell smiled. "Good."

He took her by the arm and led her around the building to a parking garage. He waved at the attendant and hit a button on his key chain. A black Saab honked its horn and flashed its lights.

"Hail to the chief," Dell said with a wink.

Margery continued to frown as he led her to his car and opened her door. He jogged around to the driver's side, climbed in, and slid his key into the ignition. Margery stared straight ahead, but she could feel his smile beaming towards her.

"Where to?"

"I live on the north side," she said, slouching in her seat.

Dell let out a low whistle. "Really? That's a long commute to Blues. You bet on horses often? Because I swear I've seen you there before."

"I'm there often enough," Margery said, adjusting her seat belt.

Dell laughed. "Me, too," he said.

As the Saab rolled out of the garage and onto the blissful streets of suburbia, Margery fixed her eyes out the window at the peaceful neighborhood of pretty houses, golden retrievers, and happy families. She longed to press her face against the glass to feel the smooth texture of the good life that lay just out of her reach. Instead she balled her hands into fists and pressed them against the plush interior of the car.

"So what do you do besides bet on horses?" Dell asked after clicking on the radio to an all jazz station.

Margery sniffed. "I work for a cleaning service."

"I thought I detected the lovely scent of lemon fresh," he said with a chuckle.

She didn't flinch. "I only work when they call me, and they don't call me very often," she said.

"Oh? And why is that?"

"Because I'm a terrible housekeeper," she said.

Dell raised his eyebrows. "Well, that would be a problem..."

Margery shrugged. "Yeah, but they have some clients they don't like so much. They save me for those jobs."

"Poor fools," Dell said. "What cleaning service do you work for? I'll be sure to keep it in mind if I ever have a client I want to piss off."

"Dust Bunnies," Margery said.

"Dust Bunnies? Isn't that the one where the cleaning girls have to dress up?"

"Yes," she said.

Dell laughed. "You don't seem too bothered by it."

"By what?" She stared out the window at a family flopped in the snow making snow angels.

"The costume, the job..."

"Why should it bother me?" she asked.

Dell's face puckered in surprise. "I guess it would bother me."

"Oh," she said.

"Well, do you have a family? A boyfriend?" Dell pressed.

"Occasionally," she said.

"Occasionally," he repeated. "I'm just not going to find anything out, am I?"

Margery glanced at him out of the corner of her eye. "Seems that you've found out everything you've asked."

Dell started to say something else but opted for silence. Margery sniffed again. She fixed her eye on the street and absorbed the painful transition from paradise to purgatory with the dissipation of built-to-last homes to ramshackle barracks for the socially branded. She bit her lip and closed her eyes, displacing the warm spice smell of the Saab with the gritty, sweat-soaked smell of home.

"At the next light, turn right. I live in Amityville Village Apartments, on the right just past that Dairy Mart," she muttered, her eyes still closed.

"Amityville? Like the movie?" Dell asked.

"Scarier than the movie," she said, an insincere smile flitting across her face. "Much scarier."

"OK," he said, pulling into the gravel parking lot. "Home sweet home."

"Thanks for the ride," she said, her hand on the door.

He reached across and caught her arm. "Margery."

She looked at him, her face grim. "Dell."

He eased his grip and smiled. "That's the first time you've said my name."

"Is it."

He nodded. "And since we're on a first name basis, I'd like to do the gentlemanly thing and walk you to your door."

"That's OK, really..."

But he was already out of the car and around to open her door. He bent and reached for her hand. She allowed herself to be helped, as he gently closed the door behind her and hit the remote lock on his key chain.

"I hate that beeping," Margery said as they walked towards the building.

"Why?" Dell asked. "Because you don't have a car with a remote lock?"

She stared straight ahead at the sagging, brown building. "Precisely."

She led him into the drab lobby with a rotting tile floor. Without looking at him, she briskly made her way through another wobbly tan door that hid the staircase. She climbed the stairs methodically, looking up at the blinking, fading lights and made a point of not touching the banister. As Dell reached for it, she swatted at his hand.

"There's a retarded man on the third floor who sometimes smears things on the banister," she said flatly. "Sometimes mayonnaise, sometimes glue, sometimes other things..."

Dell's eyes raised in disgust. "I see," he said.

She shoved her hands into her pants pockets. "You just get used to keeping your hands to yourself," she said with a shrug.

When they reached the second floor landing, she slapped the ugly tan door open and stalked down the gray hallway to apartment 2B. Glancing back, she smiled at the face that had lost its cocky air. Rapping the backside of her hand on the pea-green door, she laughed at him.

"This is me," she said.

Pulling a single key out of her back pocket, she slid it into the rusted doorknob and shoved the door open. Dell lingered in the hallway as she went in and flopped onto a patchy brown couch.

"Welcome to Shangri-La," she said, stretching her hands out along the back of the couch.

Dell stood uncomfortably in the center of the doorway. She followed his timid, almost fearful gaze around her decrepit apartment. She had almost no furnishings. Outside of the couch, her finest accommodation garnished from the street, she had a small wooden table, a beanbag chair and a tall halogen lamp. There was a small AM/FM radio that sat on the solitary window ledge and a door that led to an impossibly small bathroom. A miniature refrigerator sat beside the couch and an economy sized microwave sat on top of it. Her floor was carpeted with weeks' worth of newspapers and her wall was papered in pictures of horses and jockeys, scorecards and names. She watched in semi-amusement as Dell stepped gingerly towards the wall to get a better look at her decorations.

His eyes danced quickly from picture to picture, name to name. Turning, he pointed at her collection and opened his mouth to speak. Her eyes narrowed as he said nothing and went back to his reading.

"This is amazing, Margery," he said finally, shaking a piece of the newspaper off his foot.

"It's home," she said sullenly.

"I mean, you've got racing news from August up on this wall," he continued. "This article was in Horseracer two months ago," he said, pointing. His confident smile slowly regained its usual territory. "And this race isn't happening until next week." He turned and looked at her, his hand busily scratching his head. "You said you liked horses, but this is unbelievable!"

Margery frowned and said nothing.

Dell made his way over to the couch and plopped down beside her. He grinned and slapped his hand on her thigh. "You're my kinda woman, woman."

She rolled her eyes and folded her arms across her chest. "Gee, thanks. That makes me feel all warm and fuzzy inside."

Dell laughed and rested his hand on her knee. "What's with all the newspapers on the floor?" he asked, waving his free hand towards the ground.

"Racing news," she said. "Today's races, tomorrow's, last week's, whatever."

"Do you keep any stats?" His eyes beginning to twinkle.

"Sure," she said, nodding towards a plain black notebook on the table.

Dell picked it up and opened it to the first page.

"To Margie, from Dad. Happy birthday," he read aloud. He paused and winked at her. "This dad part of your 'occasional family,' Margie?"

Margery got up from the couch. "It's Margery. And I suppose he is," she said.

Dell began to thumb through her notes. "You've been at this for a long time. This is first dated in October of 1985."

"So?" she asked, heading towards the bathroom.

"So what did that make you -- fifteen? Sixteen?" he asked.

"I guess," she said, her hand on the bathroom door.

"My grandpa didn't start really teaching me about horses until I was eighteen. Your dad into horses?"

Margery closed the bathroom door behind her. "My father is a drunken bastard who I don't see, and I don't care to remember," she said, fishing a locked, brown box out from under the sink.

"I didn't ask for his biography, Margery," Dell said. "I asked if he was into horses."

*"Silver's Quickfoot is a winner, baby. Put your money on that horse."*

Margery closed her eyes and blinked her father's voice out of her mind. "He was into horses," she said. "I mean, I suppose he still is." She felt behind the toilet for the key to the box and opened it. Pulling the seven hundred dollars out of her pocket, she put it into the empty box and took a deep breath. Putting the box back under the sink and slipping the key back into its hiding place, she opened the door and stared at Dell, who was intently skimming her notations.

"I remember this horse -- Silver's Quickfoot," he said, jabbing his finger at the page. "My grandfather won a small fortune off of that filly."

Margery leaned against the bathroom door. "So did I."

"Yes, I can see that," Dell said, nodding in approval at the column denoting her winnings. He paused and looked up at her. "You obviously know your stuff. With your winnings, I'd think you'd live in my neighborhood..."

"Oh, don't be simple," Margery said.

"What? Patch of bad luck?" he asked.

She blinked. "I don't believe in luck."

"No, it seems that you believe in numbers," he said, resuming his reading. "Come back and sit down." He absently patted the seat beside him.

Sighing, she sat back down and patiently answered his questions about her notations, rehashed old races, discussed betting strategies and good horses. Before long, the shadows in the room were growing longer, and Margery's patience was growing shorter. Dell seemed oblivious to her discomfort as he chattered on and on about horses as he rubbed her thigh. Margery stared out the window and watched dusk settle as she drowned Dell's voice out with the sound of hooves pounding in her brain. Finally, she stood up and moved towards her refrigerator.

"I don't have much to eat, but if you insist on staying, you can take your pick," she said, opening the door to reveal stacks of frozen dinners. "I keep the setting on really cold all the time because the freezer isn't worth shit."

Dell laughed. "TV dinners?"

"I haven't got a TV," Margery said.

"Right," Dell said.

She pulled one out and opened the carton. Sliding it into the microwave, she glared at him. "Do you want one?"

He shook his head. "I'd rather learn more about the mysterious Margery. I know you love horses, but that's all I know."

"You also know where I work and that my father is a prick." She looked out the window and tapped the top of the microwave.

"That I do," he said. "But what else can you tell me? I'm fascinated by the entire package."

"Really." She turned back slowly and stared at him as she sucked in a deep breath. "My mother lives on the third floor of this building, next door to the man who's retarded. I never see her, either, because she refuses to divorce my father, who not only is a drunk but abuses her. He never laid a finger on me, but I hate him still for ruining her. And I hate her more for not getting up off the goddamn couch and leaving him. I've been on my own since I was seventeen. I dropped out of high school and never got my GED. I used to work fast food, and now I clean people's homes except basically this job is no job because they never give me any work. I used to sleep around a lot when I was younger because sometimes the guys who hung around Blues would offer to cover my bets if I, you know, helped them out, and none of them ever knew my name after they'd taken what they wanted. I was married for three months when I was nineteen to the only decent guy I ever knew in my life, but he tossed me aside because he was jealous of my horses who always came first no matter what. I haven't got any friends, I haven't got any money. I can barely afford the rent on this shit-hole apartment, if you want to know all of the details." Margery paused and stared out the window. "There is only one thing in this world that makes me happy, and it's horses."

She closed her eyes and saw the finish play of Tiyuri's win over and over again in her mind and felt the rush of excitement spread through her entire body. Opening her eyes, she felt the rush fade as quickly as it had come.

*"I love you Margie, but you're worse than a drug addict."*

Devon's words pounded her brain. She frowned and bit her lip as her eyes peeled open. She stared at Dell sitting quietly on the couch. "Devon, my ex, he was jealous that I found horse races more erotic than him, that I got a better orgasm from watching some jockey in blue pound out the home stretch. He couldn't understand." Margery's words fell off as the microwave beeped. She pulled the plastic tray out and reached into a paper bag for a plastic fork. She leaned up against the wall and blew across her food for a minute before beginning to eat. Dell stared intently at her.

Her features relaxed. "I don't drink, but I'm addicted to these painkillers I started taking after one of the men who used to fuck me broke my arm. The last guy I ever fucked for money, too. That's when I went legit and became a Dust Bunny." She paused, an ironic smile on her face. "And you thought I should be bothered by my cleaning lady uniform. You see, Dell, I'm consumed by horses. By races. I live for them. I need them more than I need food and water and certainly more than I need to see that look of absolute pity on your face." She looked him squarely in the eye, her own dark and teasing. "What about you? What's your story? Make it a good one, and I might go back to my dirty and profitable ways. That is why you offered me a ride, isn't it?"

Dell looked away. "Maybe it's time for me to go..."

She laughed. "Maybe it is."

He stood up and set her notebook back on the table. "Thanks for, uh, indulging all of my questions," he said, edging towards the door.

"You're welcome," she said.

"Well, I guess I'll see you at Blues sometime." His hand was on the door.

Margery got up slowly and walked across the room towards him. Standing close to him, she brushed her hand across his face and smiled. Pulling him even closer, she kissed him, hard, and drew back with a laugh. "Thanks for the ride, Dell."

Dell blinked and offered a half-smile. "Sure thing," he said as he slipped out the door.

She stared at the closed door until she realized she was crying. Turning, she flung herself awkwardly across the couch and sobbed into the moldy material. Her hands clutched the worn fabric, her teeth bit the old cushions. She cried into the couch until her body was exhausted by the futility of her tears. Only then did she sit up and run her finger over the neat, black covering of her racing notebook. She picked it up and hugged it close to her body. Flipping to the back cover, she found the yellowed envelope, addressed and stamped but never sent.

*To Devon. My life.*

She traced her fingers over the letters scribbled in black ink and remembered the yellow square of paper inside.

*To Devon. I'm sorry.*

She clutched the worn envelope in her fist and sniffed in the mothball scent of renewal.

*To Devon. Love, Margie.*

Margery slid the envelope back in its place and set the notebook on the table and got up. Moving slowly back into the bathroom, she pulled a bottle of Vicodin off of the sink and shook it. She had an arrangement with the male pharmacist at the corner drug store so she was always kept in supply; the bottle was nearly full.

Taking a handful into the living space of her apartment, she rolled the pills around like dice in her clenched fist. Staring out the window at the bleak, dark street, she felt her resolve diminishing. Opening her palm, she stared at the pile of pills and willed them to melt in her hand, to flow into her veins, to swim straight to her heart. She wondered how many she would have to take to surrender once and for all. Glancing up at the resolute sky, she concentrated on the trails of smoke billowing out of slender chimneys. She half-smiled as the wisps of smoke twisted and bent into the gallant form of blue horses racing towards the undiscovered country of heaven.

Heaven

*Hey monkey, don't you want
to be needed, too?*
            *"Monkey"*

He sat on his bed with his back against the wall and stared out the window at the absence of snow. It had been snowing almost nonstop the day before and almost not at all that day. He wished it wasn't dark already so he could look at the sky and see, really see, how dense the clouds were -- if there were clouds at all. He wondered what made it snow some days and not others. He wondered, he wondered.

He wondered what that lonely face across the street was doing tonight. He could see the woman in the apartment right across the street from his own staring up at the sky. Right up. He wondered what she was doing, what she was thinking. He wished he had her number, wished like hell he had her number, but all he had was his black rotary phone propped up by the thick yellow pages full of numbers of people he didn't know. He figured her name was probably listed, but he didn't know what it was, damn it, and he had no way of finding out, damn it. He wished he could get up and open the window and yell across to her, "What's your name? What's your name? Tell me so I can call you up!" but he realized even if he opened his window and yelled, her window was closed. But maybe if she saw him open his window, she'd open hers, and they could talk. He liked to talk. He loved to talk. But he didn't have anyone to talk to. Except Monkey.

Just as he was about to get up and open his window, he saw her stare at her hand and walk away from the window. He wondered if she hurt herself, wondered if she was bleeding, wondered if she was in danger. He wondered if she was reading her palm, wondered if she was trying to figure out her life, wondered if she needed as much help as he did. He leaned forward to see if he could still see her, and the muscles in his back screamed for air. He looked at the clock and realized he'd been motionless for hours, hours, just staring out the window at the Amityville Village Apartments. He was glad he didn't live in such a haunted place, such a devilish place, such a reckless, scary place. He was glad he lived in the Robert Street Apartments because Robert was a nice name, the name of his imaginary friend from grade school, and it was also a friendly sort of name, like the name of someone who would stop by for coffee or a beer. Either or, he wasn't a picky sort of guy, Robert. He was a pal, everyone's pal. Yes, he was glad he lived in Robert Street Apartments because they were newer and friendlier and didn't remind anyone of an old horror movie. He liked his home the best. It was the best on the block, on the whole north end of town. Yes, it was the best.

He tried to stand up because he realized he had to pee, but his legs were frozen, sleeping, hibernating. That's what happens when you sit motionless on a bed for hours and hours. Or maybe even days, it's hard to say, hard to measure. He didn't have much else to do but stare out the window, just stare and stare. He spent most of his time staring at the sad girl's apartment, but she was hardly ever home, so sometimes he stared at the other apartments in her building. Some of the people in Amityville Village Apartments were crazy, downright loony, insane, even. There was a guy on the third floor who would smash his face against the window and stick his tongue out at the pigeons on the roof of Robert Street Apartments, and there was an old lady on the fourth floor who walked around naked in the mornings, and there was another man on the third floor who would sometimes hit a woman with green and brown bottles, and she would never cry or try to fight back. No, she just would sit there, bleeding sometimes, while the man would wail away on her. And on the first floor, there was a prostitute who would dress like a policewoman and handcuff men to the bars on her windows. He knew she was a prostitute because she'd told him. Her name was Phyllis. He met her on the street once when he was going to the store to buy some cigarettes and comic books. She'd stopped him and asked him what he was doing and would he like a twirl and he'd said, "Twirl? Like a leaf to the ground?" and she'd said, "Something like that" and he'd laughed and walked away. He knew a lot about prostitutes because his grandmother had been one back in the fifties before she'd had his mother, and it skipped a generation since his sister was now a prostitute, but his mother had never been one. He'd asked his sister once if she knew Phyllis, and she had hung up the phone on him.

He inched himself to the edge of his bed and tried to wiggle his toes. He could tell it would be awhile before they broke their slumber, so he flopped back on his bed and smacked his head against the wall. Rubbing his skull, he turned his head towards the phone and picked it up. He dialed quickly, and it rang four times.

A child answered. "Hello?"

He cleared his throat and said, "Is this heaven?"

There was a pause. "This is the Roberts."

He raised his eyebrows. "Ya don't say? Roberts? A house full of them?"

After another short pause, he heard the phone clatter down, and the dial tone blared in his ear. He turned his body to the side and continued to wiggle his toes, but, damn it, his legs were asleep still, damn it. He put the phone down and flipped the yellow pages open. Without paying attention to names, he dialed the first number he saw.

"Hello?" The voice sounded tired.

"Yes, is this heaven?" he asked.

"What?"

"Is this heaven?" he repeated.

"No, this is Dante's Inferno," the voice said before hanging up.

He put the phone back in its cradle and wiggled his toes again. He turned the radio on, but it was that annoying commercial, damn annoying, about Burt's Carpet Factory, so he turned it off. He was beginning to feel the tingle spread through his body. He wondered what he should do when he got up -- should he pee first or eat first? No, he should look for Monkey. He wasn't sure when he'd last seen her, but he knew it had been awhile. Monkey always stayed hidden, always, always, it was like she was afraid of the light of day. Except it was night. He sat up and whistled.

"Monkey! Come here, Monkey!" he called softly.

No response.

He flipped over on his stomach and hung his head under the bed. He grinned at the shining pair of deep metallic blue eyes that were staring back at him. He reached under and pulled the dark gray tabby cat out from her hiding place.

"Monkey, that's where you've been hiding," he said, tumbling off the bed and onto the floor beside her. "I've been looking for you for days and days."

Monkey responded by dashing back under the bed.

He grinned and hopped to his feet. "Well, Monkey's still alive. Must be OK."

He ambled into the bathroom and stuck his tongue out at the crude reflection. He had never been considered handsome, not even by Phyllis, but he had a raw energy about him that used to drive the girls wild on the playground. He was tall and wiry, his eyes big and bloodshot and brown, his head was an odd oblong shape, and his hair was buzzed to the quick. His skin was pale but blotchy because contact with Monkey made him break out in hives, but he loved the old cat and couldn't get rid of her, not even for his own well-being. He would never get rid of Monkey. She loved him and needed him, and he would never let her down. Never never ever.

He grinned at his reflection as he made his way to the toilet. Standing there, peeing, he wondered if maybe he should have eaten first, maybe he should have eaten something good and spent some time with Monkey, but, hell, he was already peeing, so what could you do about that? After he finished, he flushed and washed his hands and winked at his reflection.

As he started down the short, softly carpeted hallway to the kitchen to get something to eat, he wondered what it was like to be blind, and he closed his eyes and stuck his hands straight out in front of him, right the hell out in front. He got about three steps and stubbed his toe on his pile of comics and another two steps and smashed his fingers into the wall. It must be awful to be blind, he decided, as he opened his eyes and went into the kitchen. He was sure hungry. He couldn't remember the last time he'd remembered to eat. He thought maybe yesterday, during the snow, he'd taken a break and gotten up to eat. But maybe it had been two days, it's hard to say. He opened up his refrigerator and stared at the head of rotting lettuce that sat on the top shelf, and he wondered why he didn't put it in the crisper until he remembered he'd pulled that drawer out to give Monkey a proper litter box, and he cursed the decision as he stared at the rotting head of lettuce. It was all he had left, besides a jar of mayonnaise, which he also pulled out. He carried the lettuce and the mayonnaise with him back to his bedroom and he climbed back up on his bunk bed, he called it his bunk bed since Monkey slept beneath where he slept, and tore a piece of the lettuce off. Dipping it in the jar of mayonnaise and sliding it into his mouth, he ignored the uncrispness of the lettuce and wondered if he hadn't stumbled upon a great culinary innovation: mayolettucenaise, head-o-naise, lettuce-*con*-mayo. He flipped open the yellow pages and considered calling a few restaurants, but he decided not to. Not until he'd thought of a good name, a great name, a killer name, a boppo name. A name to end all names. A culinary feat needed such a name.

He crunched slowly on his let-us-eat-mayonnaise and picked up the phone again. He glanced in the open phone book and dialed.

"Hello?" the voice asked in a thick Hispanic accent.

"Is this heaven, by chance?" he asked.

"Heaven? Like the strip club?"

"No, no. Like heaven -- as in heaven," he explained.

The voice laughed. "No, *hombre*. Wrong number, OK?"

"Oh, I'm sorry to have bothered you."

"*No problema*," the voice said before the dial tone began to blare.

He stared out the window again and wished it was day time. Life was clearer in the day, much clearer. He turned on the radio.

"*Ain't no sunshine when she's gone...*"

Ain't that the truth! He missed the sun already, missed the day, missed the girl he'd never had. He rolled over on his stomach and slid so his head touched the ground.

"Monkey? Why don't you come out and play," he said.

The cat stared back at him and said nothing.

He tumbled off the bed and picked up his food. He guessed he was done. He guessed he'd have to think about what to call his new dish some other time. He guessed that he should go to bed. It wasn't very late, but he figured his sister was probably out prowling around with Phyllis and that was his cue to sleep.

He stumbled back into the kitchen and discovered again why he never wanted to be a blind man and then skipped back to bed. He propped himself up against the wall and put his hand on the phone in case someone might call. One could never quite tell when his phone might ring. So he was always ready. He had on his best pair of jeans in case

Robert called to invite him out for a night on the town. Well, not Robert, necessarily, but someone like Robert. The personification of Monkey, perhaps. He wasn't particular. He leaned his head against the wall and waited. And waited.

And waited.

The sun rose up the next morning and faded the next night, and he went through his usual routine of opening the phone book, dialing the number, and asking:

"Is this heaven?"

He was a patient man, and he didn't care how many people hung up on him, cursed him, berated him, laughed at him, screamed at him, chided him, goaded him, played with him, lied to him. He knew one day, one day, one day, he'd find it. The number. The direct line to God. He'd find it. And wouldn't They all be jealous then. Day after day after week after day, he searched for the number. He searched as the snow whipped against his window, as the man beat the woman with the bottles, as the old lady walked around naked, as Monkey hid under the bed, as Phyllis tried to grab his penis when he stood in line to buy cigarettes and comic books, as the light of the sun was replaced by the glow of the street light, as the snow melted away, as the snow returned, as the snow melted away again, and so on and so on and so on. He lived to find God, to find God, to find heaven. He lived to prove his grandmother wrong when she said, "God is the circus clown swinging on the trapeze between my tits," he lived to prove her wrong, he knew she was wrong. He knew his mother was right when she said, "God is in heaven and He's there for you to talk to anytime – anytime -- about anything. Just call on Him and He'll be there, just for you." He knew his mother was right and his grandmother was wrong. He knew it. But every day, he stared out the window and tried to think of the number, what was that number, and wished his mother hadn't drowned in the pool at the Y because he bet that she knew the number. Every day, he dialed and dialed and dialed. No heaven, not today.

"Hey, Monkey," he said one day. "Am I awake right now? Am I dreaming? Am I even still alive?"

Monkey stared at him from under the bed and said nothing.

"Do you think I'm even alive? What if I'm not? What if I'm dead? How would I know? You'd tell me, right, if I was dead? Anyone else would let me go on thinking I was alive even if I was dead, but I know that you wouldn't."

Monkey yawned.

Yes, Monkey would tell him. Monkey understood him better than anyone else. Monkey would help him. He knew it, just as sure as he knew that his grandmother was wrong about God.

He was lonely, so lonely, so lonely. He wondered if he should go out more but the only place he needed to go was to buy his cigarettes and comic books. Cigarettes, which he never smoked but delivered with reverence to his aging grandmother, and comic books he never read, but stacked in his hallway. He loved to stack things, he loved the way it looked. It was like rings in a tree trunk, told him how long he'd lived, how much he'd lived. Made him feel proud and lucky to be alive, his comic book collection. His grandmother always answered the door to her apartment in her bathrobe, hooked up to an oxygen tank, with a cigarette hanging dangerously out of her mouth, calling him a twenty-two-year-old baby for wasting his allowance on comic books. Every week, he'd stare at her feet and tell her, tell her, that she'd kill herself with that cigarette and that oxygen tank, but she told him to shut up, just shut up, monkey-boy, and she'd slam the door, except for every four weeks when she'd hand him an envelope of money to give to his landlady, a friend of his grandmother's.

He hated going out to see his grandmother, hated the sting of fresh air against his pale, blotchy face, hated the contact with his feet on the pavement. He liked his apartment, liked his bed, liked his stack of comics, liked his quest, his crusade, for God. No, he didn't want to go out more. Didn't need to. Even though he was lonely, so lonely, and spiraling down into a sea of self-loathing that could only be comforted by a friend, a real friend, not just Monkey.

Day after day after week after day he picked up the phone and dialed, picked up the phone and dialed, picked up the phone and dialed. One day in very early spring, he dialed and, after hello, he said:

"Is this heaven?"

And a deep, resonating voice replied, "Yes."

His ears pricked up in earnest as he asked, "Heaven as in God's house?"

"Yes."

He felt his pulse quicken. "No shit. Heaven as in heaven?"

"That's right."

"Is this God?"

"Speaking."

"This is wonderful! I've finally found you!"

"I was always here, my son."

"Right," he said. Smiling and casual, he hung up the phone and turned on the radio.

*"She's a brick and I'm drowning slowly..."*

He cocked his head to the side and felt sorry for Ben Folds 5, sorry for sad old Ben, because he was elated, rising, spinning, singing, dancing, laughing, springing, praying, happier than limits allowed, the antithesis of drowning. He rolled off the bed and pulled Monkey out from her hiding spot.

"I found God," he said, scratching her ears.

She looked at him and said nothing.

"I found God!" he repeated, jumping to his feet. Monkey dashed back under the bed.

Opening the yellow pages, he scanned the restaurant ads and punched the number into his phone.

"Hello, this is Grubs. How can I help?" the voice said.

"Two things," he began. "First, I have an idea for a new appetizer called Lettuce-n-mayo Wilted Crispers, and second, God exists -- I've found Him. Have you?"

Stunned silence was his reply.

Grubs

*I been bummin' around this old town*
*for way, way, way, way, way too long*
*"Hanginaround"*

"God exists -- I've found Him.  Have you?"

Manny clutched the phone in his thick, sweaty hands and rubbed his free hand through his disheveled hair.  "Uh..."

"Keep looking.  You'll find Him," the voice said.  "Proves that mothers are right and grandmothers are wrong."

"Huh?" Manny asked.

"Never mind.  Back to my idea about the appetizer..."

"Yeah, listen, buddy, why don't you call back when the manager's available."

"I will.  When would be a good time?"

"Robert will be here in an hour."

"Robert?" the voice asked.

"Yeah, he's the manager," Manny said.

"How wonderful, really wonderful.  Tell Robert I'll call him later," the voice said.

"Sure thing," Manny said as he hung up the phone.  "Must be Crazy Thursday," he muttered.

"Hey, Manuel, can I get a Mudslide and two Buds for Table 15?" a waitress asked, tapping her long white nails on the polished bar.

"Sure, Diane," he said, still shaking his head.

She smiled.  "What's the matter?"

"I just got a call from some religious nut who wanted to know if I'd found God yet."

"And all this time I thought we were supposed to be looking for Jesus," Diane said with a chuckle.

They looked at each other and said in unison, "It must be Crazy Thursday."

Diane set her tray on the bar and tugged at the floppy white ribbon tying back her straight blond hair with fire-red streaks. "I've got a rowdy bunch tonight, myself," she said. "Nobody claiming to be angels or circus clowns, but it's still early."

Manny set the drinks on her tray. "Why do we put up with this job?" he asked.

She shrugged. "Because Grubs is the finest eatery in all of Northeastern Ohio?"

Manny raised a suspicious eyebrow. "Nooo... I don't think that's it."

She picked the tray up. "Because we're working-class gluttons for punishment?"

Manny nodded slowly. "At least that's what the bumper sticker on my Benz says."

Diane laughed and maneuvered through the jungle of tables pushed too close together. Stopping at a small circular table in almost the exact center of the restaurant, she took the drinks off her tray and set them before three slightly drunk men.

"Need anything else, gentlemen?" Diane asked, pressing her tray flat against her black t-shirt.

"From you?" asked a boyish-looking man with curly black hair and brilliant green eyes. "Where to begin..."

"You could cut my meat for me," said the man with the Mudslide.

"Dober, Talbot, leave the woman alone," the third said. Standing, he offered her his hand. "I'm Greg Graginski. Can I buy you a drink?"

Diane backed up a step. "Uh..."

"Or you could just write your phone number in ketchup across my hamburger when you bring it out," Talbot offered, stirring his drink.

Dober reached over and pulled an empty chair away from a nearby table and set it next to himself. Brushing his black hair out of his eyes, he winked at her. "You can sit with us for awhile, right? It's not too busy right now."

Diane glanced over at the bar and saw that Manny was busy making a drink for a pretty blond. Looking back at the expecting eyes of the three drunken patrons, she smiled weakly. "I'm on the clock, fellas..."

"Listen, Diane," Graginski said, squinting at her nametag. "We can appreciate how hard you must work here. On your feet all the time, you know. All we're saying is maybe you'd like to take a break."

"And we'd love it if such a pretty waitress would take her much-deserved break with us," Dober said.

Talbot stirred his drink. "I just want her to cut my meat," he mumbled.

"Shut up," Dober growled.

Talbot sucked the alcohol up through a straw. "Fine," he said.

Dober nodded towards Diane. "You work out?" he asked.

"I like to jog," she said warily.

"I can tell." Dober winked. "I like a woman who takes care of herself," he said.

Diane rolled her eyes. "I get that," she said.

"You see, Diane, it's these blue lights you guys have in here. They make us a little randy. We were sitting around Dober's apartment doing shots of tequila, but his apartment is all white. His old lady's into modern art and so everything is white -- the couch, the walls, the curtains. And all that white was giving us a headache," Graginski explained.

"So we came here because we think we look better under the blue lights," Dober continued.

"And because the waitresses are cute," Talbot added.

Diane took another step back. "It was nice of you guys to offer, but I think the blue lights make you look like Smurfs. And you know what they say about Smurfs... They have small feet. Enjoy your drinks!" she said, walking away.

"What does she expect? Smurfs are only three apples high," Talbot murmured.

"Small feet," Graginski grumbled. "I don't have no small feet!" he yelled at her retreating figure.

Dober laughed and chugged his beer. "Did you know that the Smurfs are Communist propaganda?"

"Get out," Talbot said.

"No, really. Think about it. They all look the same and dress the same. And who are the characters? Hefty and Handy, the soldier and the worker. Clearly representative of the important pieces of a classless, worker-centered society."

Graginski and Talbot leaned in towards Dober in interest. "That's deep," Talbot said.

"Oh, but there's more evidence yet!" Dober said, waving a finger in the air. "Who are the other characters? Greedy, Vanity, and Brainy. Greedy is a taker who contributes nothing to the system; he just eats all the time. Vanity is too concerned with looks to be functional, and Brainy is a weak intellectual who contributes only abstract things to the Smurfian utopia. They are all obviously symbols of what breaks down the system. And Papa Smurf! How can you miss his symbolism? He's the only one who looks different from the rest of those Commies. And what color does he wear?"

"Red..." Graginski leaned back in his chair with his hand pressed against his face. "Hot damn."

Dober nodded slowly. "That's right. Papa Smurf, Joseph Stalin, same diff."

"But what about the cat and the dude?" Talbot asked uncertainly.

"Asreal and Gargamel? Think about it, Talbot. What's the biggest threat to the Commies?"

"The Berlin Wall?" Talbot asked, scratching his head.

Dober groaned. "No, the Communists biggest enemy was not a wall."

"It wasn't? Then what was the big deal about tearing it down?" Talbot asked.

Dober stared at him. "Forget the Berlin Wall," he said. "The biggest threats to the Communists were the Capitalists. The West. Us!"

"So you're saying when we were cheering for the Smurfs to get away from the cat and the dude, we were cheering for the Commies?"

Dober nodded. "We were cheering for a classless society full of equal prosperity for all of the workers that was lead by a 3-apple-high blue man in a red uniform."

"That doesn't sound too bad..." Talbot said, stirring his drink.

"But don't you see? It *is* bad," Dober said. "Communism is bad. I mean, it fails as a system because it supports a utopian philosophy that is unrealistic and irrational."

"Utopia?" Talbot asked.

"Perfect world, dip-shit," Dober said dismissively. "We can't have our kids watching the Smurfs and being brainwashed by the Communist ideals imbedded within the show."

"Dude, I don't think the show's actually even on anymore," Talbot said.

"It's on the Cartoon Network..." Dober said defensively.

"I can't believe the Smurfs were Communists..." Graginski said, shaking his head. He paused and looked at Dober. "How did you find all of this out? Was there something on CNN? Was there an expose on Dateline?"

Dober stared at his empty beer glass. "No, it was a forward this guy I work with e-mailed me."

Graginski and Talbot looked at each other, a slow smirk rising on their faces. Dober squinted at the foam on the bottom of his glass.

"Who says you can't learn anything from a forward?" Talbot said with a laugh. "I learned that Marilyn Monroe wore a size 14 in one my kid sister sent me."

Dober narrowed his eyes. "Shut up."

"The Smurfs are Communist... And you know because of e-mail." Talbot began to laugh loudly. "That's rich, McCarthy," he said through his nose.

"He knows who McCarthy is but he doesn't know 'utopia'..." Dober mumbled.

Graginski started laughing, too. "Hey, just because McCarthy was a political joke doesn't mean that he was wrong."

Dober shifted in his chair. "I'm just telling you what I heard," he muttered.

"Well, if it isn't Mark Dober, bonded in marriage but still out living the high life," a voice said behind them.

Dober turned his head to the side. "Ted Dobbins, the man whose claim to fame is graduating high school ahead of me -- alphabetically." He grinned and stood up. "How are you, Teddy?"

"I'm doing pretty well," Ted said, shaking his hand.

"Why don't you sit for a second?" Dober said, offering him the empty chair they'd acquired for Diane.

Ted glanced around. "For a second. I have a date here."

"I miss the single days," Dober said wistfully.

"Now we're the hottest dates he's allowed to have," Graginski said.

Ted grinned. "How are you, Greg? Talbot?"

"I was doing great until I found out the Smurfs were a bunch of Communists," Talbot said slyly.

"What?" Ted asked.

"Never mind," Dober muttered.

"Hey, are you here with CeCe, Ted?" Graginski asked, glancing around.

"Oh, no. We broke up awhile ago," Ted said. "I'm actually on a first date with a friend's girlfriend's roommate."

"Does your date have short brown hair, killer body?" Graginski asked.

Ted nodded. "She does. Why do you ask?"

"Because she's sitting over on the couches with CeCe," he replied.

"Holy shit!" Ted stood up quick enough to teeter the chair.

"*Vaya con dios*," Graginski called after him.

Ted hurried over to the platformed area near the bar where three large blue couches hugged the wall. Sure enough, CeCe, wearing black fishnet stockings, red leather skirt, and a loose-fitting black top, was sitting on the middle couch next to his date. Groaning inwardly, he fidgeted with his clothes and stepped up on the platform. CeCe was laughing and so was his date.

"Marci, let's go sit at the bar," he said.

His date, a clean-cut brunette wearing pinstripe black pants and a white sleeveless shirt, smiled at him. "I like the couches, Ted. They're so much cozier." She patted the seat next to her.

CeCe slid over. "No, Ted, sit here," she said, patting the space between the women.

Ted stood awkwardly for a moment before sitting down between them, his face burning bright red. "So..." he said.

Marci grinned. "I was telling CeCe here all about you," she said.

Ted's face dropped. "Really."

CeCe smiled. "Marci likes your cologne," she said.

Ted moaned and put his face in his hands. "Really."

"I didn't tell her that I gave that cologne to you on our last anniversary," CeCe said with a yawn. "I wanted her to think it was something special you picked up just for her."

Marci's smile faded. "You didn't mention you knew him..."

CeCe tucked her feet up under her. "Oh, yes."

Marci narrowed her eyes. "Oh."

"I just wanted to come over and say hi and see who the next unfortunate sap was going to be," CeCe said, waving her hand aimlessly. "My advice, Marci, is not to push old Ted here past the friendship breaking point. Because he's not so good at intimacy."

"CeCe, please..." Ted said, taking his hands away from his face and balling them in his lap.

"Don't be so anal, Teddy," CeCe said. She leaned across his lap and looked Marci in the eye. "When I say he's not good at intimacy, I mean that he can't communicate so well. Physically he's, well, above average. I'd say solid B or B+. But when it comes to talking about anything that isn't something you would discuss with a perfect stranger at a bus stop in the ghetto in the middle of the night, Ted fails. F. Fails." CeCe leaned back to her own seat.

Marci looked suspiciously between her date and his ex. "Oh," she said.

Ted stood up and grabbed CeCe's arm. "Time to go," he said.

CeCe remained in her seat. "No. I just have one more thing to say and then I can leave you and Little Miss Muffet here alone."

Ted let go of her arm and stood in front of her. "What."

CeCe stood up slowly and ran her hand along his arm. Smiling sadly, she pressed her body against his and whispered in his ear. "I'm glad I ran into you again, Teddy, because I just had to tell you the most exciting news. Last night, I had the best sex of my life. A-plus-plus. And it was so great because it wasn't with you." She pulled back from him, a stubborn tear peeking out of the corner of her eye. "I wish you could have loved me just a little bit more, Ted, that's all," she said.

Ted's eyes darted from CeCe's face to Marci's. "Please say good-bye, CeCe."

She bit her lip and nodded slowly, her eyes drifting from Ted to the floor. "Right," she said.

"Hey, when's the band going to get here?" a voice called from the bar.

CeCe, Ted, and Marci all turned their heads to look at a perky young blond in glitter jeans and a white tank top perched on top of a bar stool. Ted squinted.

"Is that Vikki?" he asked.

CeCe frowned. "Yes," she said.

"Sitting at the bar..." he said.

"So it seems," she said.

Ted raised his eyebrows. "Oh," he said.

CeCe drew in a shaky breath. "Good-bye, Teddy," she muttered as she stepped off the platform. She moved quickly to the bar where she sat down on the stool next to Vikki.

"Hey, CeCe!" she said, giggling.

CeCe tapped her fingers on the bar and nodded at the bartender. Manny came over and smiled at her. "Haven't seen you for a little while. What can I get you?" he asked.

"What did you get for her, Manny?" she asked, nodding at her friend.

Manny thought for a moment. "She ordered a couple different kinds of shots and a fuzzy navel," he said.

CeCe nodded slowly. "OK," she said.

Manny raised a wary eyebrow. "Anything for you?" he asked.

CeCe shook her head. "No."

Vikki rocked on the bar stool. "Leave Manny alone, Ceese," she said. "He's an innocent bystander."

CeCe turned and looked at Vikki. "And who are you? The drive-by shooter?"

Vikki exploded in giggles. "Bang bang!"

Manny eyed them. "Let me know if you ladies need anything," he said, moving away and muttering, "Crazy Thursday."

She put a gentle hand on Vikki's arm. "Vik, let me take you home," she said.

Vikki's smile was lopsided. "I'm waiting for the band," she said.

CeCe sighed. "You need to get out of here."

Vikki narrowed her eyes. "You need to get out of my face, CeCe."

CeCe tapped her fingers on the counter. "You know I can't do that -- that I won't."

Vikki rocked on her seat. "Quit trying to save me, Ceese. Really."

CeCe looked between Vikki and Ted, who was brushing his hand across Little Miss Muffet's face. Shaking her head, she blew out a defeated gust of breath and stood up. "Hey, Manny," she called.

Manny turned towards her. "Yo!" he said.

"Don't serve her anymore," she said, pointing at Vikki.

Manny hesitated. "Uh..."

"Really," CeCe said. "I mean it."

Manny blinked. "OK."

Vikki glared at her friend. "I just want to hear the band," she said.

CeCe climbed off the bar stool and frowned at Vikki. "Did you drive?"

Vikki shook her head. "I walked. It was so nice, like it used to be..."

CeCe half-smiled. "It's spring, Vik."

Vikki grinned. "No, I mean, it's so nice like it used to be. Like when it was you and Teddy, me and Mikey. 'member?"

CeCe nodded. "Of course I do..."

Vikki's face crumpled. "What happened?"

CeCe shook her head. "I'm still there for you anytime, Vikki. All you have to do is call." She paused. "I've missed you at AA," she said.

Vikki's eyes shot up to meet CeCe's. "I've been busy," she mumbled.

CeCe smiled sadly. "Yeah," she said.

The two friends were quiet for a moment, each waiting for the other to speak. Finally, CeCe said, "You're sure you can get home OK?"

Vikki nodded. "I just want to hear the band," she said again.

CeCe stared at her. "Sure."

Turning, CeCe headed out the door. Vikki spun around in her seat to face the rows of alcohol on the bar. She swallowed thickly and signaled Manny.

"Can I get a rum and Coke?" she asked.

Manny shook his head. "How about a plain Coke?" he asked.

Vikki looked past him to the bottles of liquor. "Make it diet," she mumbled.

"You got it," he said.

Without waiting for him to get her the drink, she moved to the platform on the opposite side of the bar from the couches. The DJ was moving some of his equipment out of the way to make room for the band. Vikki sat on the floor and watched him work. She became enchanted with the simple movements of his body, mesmerized by his seamless fluidity, and felt a trance-like meditation fall over her. With her eyes half-closed, she thought about the alcohol dancing through her blood stream and winced. Chewing on a strand of her blond hair, she wished she had a leech to suck the poison out of her, wished she had a filter to rid her body of the need to replenish the poison even after the leech was done.

"Hey, here's your drink," a quiet voice said.

Opening her eyes, she saw Manny crouched beside her, her Diet Coke in hand.

"Thanks." She took the drink from him and set it on the ground.

"You a fan?" he asked, nodding towards the now-empty stage.

"They're my favorite band," she said with a flat smile.

Manny stood up. "Enjoy," he said, heading back to his station.

Vikki closed her eyes and leaned against the hardwood of the bar. In the back of her mind, she saw CeCe's disappointed face and cringed. Feeling herself slip to the floor, she lay with her head beside the stage and felt the alcohol effervesce through her brain as CeCe's image turned grainy and blew away like dust. Opening her eyes an undisclosed amount of time later, she stared up the pant leg of a man with a bass guitar.

"Oh!" she said, remaining flat on the floor. "You're here!"

The man with the guitar looked down. "Uh, yeah," he said.

"Where have you been? I've been lying right here on the floor waiting for you," she said with a grin.

The man grinned back, his shaggy brown hair shadowing his face. "Then I should have gotten here earlier," he said.

Vikki sat up and rested her elbows on the platform. "Play me a good song," she said, her eyes half-closed. "Something happy."

The man nodded. "Sure thing," he said.

Vikki giggled. "You're cute," she said.

"Excuse me, miss?" a voice said behind her.

Vikki turned to glance up at a waitress who had blond hair with red streaks. "Yeah?"

"Can I get you anything?" she asked.

Vikki grinned. "He's taking care of it," she said, nodding towards the stage.

"Sure he is," she said, swinging back over towards the bar.

Manny grinned as Diane plopped down on a barstool. "Crazy Thursday," he said with a shrug. "What can you do?"

Diane rubbed a tired hand across her forehead. "What makes Thursdays like this?" she asked. "I mean, the guys at Table 15 are talking about Communist propaganda, the girls at Booth 3 are talking about their boyfriends' mothers and Oedipus complexes, the couple at Table 13 are discussing the artistry of WWF wrestling costumes and make up, and the couple over there on the couches is swapping ex-fiancé horror stories. I heard the woman say she was actually engaged to a polygamist!" Diane paused and shook her head. "And that girl sitting over there on the floor is looking to get some, uh, guitar lessons from my brother."

Manny glanced over at Vikki, engrossed in a quiet study of the bass player. "Pete can't help it that Rotten Cucumbers happens to be her favorite band," he said with a laugh.

"She thinks they're so great, she should live in my mother's basement where they practice," Diane said.

"Sounds like fun to me."

"Spoken like a man who's never lived in my mother's basement," she said dryly.

Manny laughed and rested his elbows on the bar. "Guilty."

Diane rolled her shoulders. "I'm feeling guilty," she said.

"About...?"

She patted her flat stomach. "Been slacking on the exercise," she said.

"Oh, it shows," Manny said, patting his own rounded belly.

She grinned. "Those jackasses at 15 reminded me how lax I've been on my workouts when they were trying pathetically to hit on me." She shook her head and laughed. "Really, though, I need to get back into running. It's the best way to relieve my stress. But between working here and going to class, I barely have time to sleep."

"You're graduating soon, though, right?"

She nodded. "I have a couple classes I'm taking this summer and I'll be done..."

"And free to work here full time," Manny added slyly.

She rolled her eyes. "I think I'll jog across the country like Forrest Gump," she said.

Manny laughed. "That's the best way to make use of your liberal arts degree."

She glanced around at the nearly-full bar and sighed. Rubbing her temple, she sighed and said, "How much longer until we can get out of here?"

Manny shrugged. "We've been hanging around too long to leave anytime soon."

Diane lay her head on the bar and moaned as Rotten Cucumber began to tune up.

Make Like a Tree

*You go to sleep dreaming how you would
be a different kind if you thought you could
but come awake they way you are instead
"All My Friends"*

His feet shuffled along the dirt path as he whistled a song from his youth. Something about bluebells in April. Or was it rosebuds in May? Tilting his head upwards, his eyes inspected the rows of tree branches above him. He smiled, an almost goofy, giddy smile, and, spinning halfway around, stretched his hands out to his side. He was feeling lighthearted, master of this fragment in time. He stopped his dance as a jogger appeared around the bend. Feeling foolish, he stuffed his hands into his pocket and leaned against a tree. The jogger, a sweaty blond with red streaks in her hair, came closer and passed without even looking in his direction. He was momentarily mesmerized by the trails of fire vaporizing from the red streaks. Shaking himself out of his daze, he headed through the wake of her dust storm.

Garbo Proctor had found his heaven in these woods, alone with nature, his own kingdom. As a child, he and his friend Roger had launched bottle rockets in Marshall Johnson Field at the mouth of the trail, and as a lovesick teenager, he'd brought his beloved Sally Stube on this sun-splattered pathway in attempts to woo her. As he walked along the path now, surrounded by a fortress of trees, he resumed his whistling and wondered where Roger and Sally were now. He had long since forgotten to think of them and scratched his head at his vain attempt to recall those days now.

The mid-afternoon sun darted through the canopy of leaves and created a kaleidoscope on the path. Garbo couldn't help but two-step his way through the maze of light and shadow, never wanting to ruin the perfect pattern implemented by the angles of the light and the rustling of the breeze through the branches. He wished he had brought his camera because these shapes would be ideal for his portfolio. It was one of the few times in fifteen years he had left his apartment without his camera. On his self-declared day off, he had come to Marshall Johnson Field to walk on the trails and nothing more. Crouching on the dirt path, though, Garbo traced his fingers along the sharp edge of one of the darker shadows.

"Woulda made a great photograph," he murmured.

Shrugging, he stood up and swiped his foot over his tracing. By the time anyone else ventured past this spot, his lines would be obsolete. He smiled again, in awe of the power of nature. He closed his eyes and drew in a deep breath. The smell of spring flowers and new grass filled his anxious nostrils. He had learned that if he stood very still, he could hear the beauty around him. He had a recurring dream in which he stood in the middle of this very path, and Mother Nature herself came and spoke to him. It was a silly dream, he knew that, but he always half-convinced himself that if he remained quiet, then maybe he'd open his eyes and his dream would come true.

Garbo was lonely by most men's standards. He needed his dreams.

It was his thirty-third birthday. As far as he knew, no one had remembered. Even when he was a child and people took the time to remember and plan parties and buy presents, they always seemed to forget his birthday. He wished he could shrug away the memories, but he couldn't.

One birthday in particular stood out for him. It was his seventeenth. His father had been out of town and was three days late paying his respects. His mother remembered around seven o'clock that evening and rushed out to buy a gallon of rocky road. But none of that is what stuck with him. None of that made the day any different from any other birthday.

His friend Steve, his ride to school, had a beat-up truck with worn-out shocks and springs jutting through the seats. Every day, Roger sat in the cab with Steve, while Garbo opted for the bed of the truck. As soon as the good-morning grunts were over, they argued over the radio, Steve voting for country, Roger voting for sports talk, and Garbo wishing for jazz. As usual, the argument ended with Steve stubbornly shoving his weary old tape of the Doors in the tape deck. Why it mattered so much, Garbo never understood. The ride to school was always over before it began.

But not on his seventeenth birthday.

That was the day that Steve got a flat tire, and the three boys had to walk the final three blocks to the high school. As they walked, Garbo kicked a rock. Step-step-kick. Step-step-kick. Step-step-kick.

"Hey, Garbo, why doncha quit that?" Roger said.

He looked sideways at his friend. "Why?"

"Dunno. It's annoying."

Steve snickered and seized the opportunity. He raced out in front of them and kicked the rock himself. Garbo grinned sheepishly at Roger. Steve turned and faced them, lining the rock in front of him.

"Time to give this rock a ride!" he yelled as he kicked it towards them.

The rock skidded across the pavement and deflected off Roger's shoe.

"Watch it!" He kicked the rock back.

Garbo watched his friends chase off down the block, arguing and cussing. He considered chasing after them, but the day was too beautiful to run through. His pace slowed until he was barely even moving.

"You know, Garbo, you're never going to make it before the first bell at that pace."

It was Sally Stube. His Sally. She was standing next to him.

His palms got sweaty.

"If I'm late, I'm late," he said.

She smiled and her blond ponytail bobbed slightly as she turned her head towards him. "Well, I'm never late, so stick with me, OK?" She slid her arm through his.

"Sure."

They walked in silence, Sally hugging Garbo's arm close to her. She smelled like vanilla.... or cinnamon. He couldn't tell which. He wished he had Steve's ability to say something witty or Roger's way of knowing just how to move his body. All he had, though, was his eyes.

When they were in the parking lot of the high school, Sally loosed her arm from the crutch of his elbow and turned to face him.

"Thanks for walking me to school, Garbo," she said.

"Garbo! There you are!"

It was Steve, yelling from across the lot.

Garbo raised his hand slightly to indicate he heard him. Sally turned towards the racket and shook her head.

"That boy..." she said, her cheeks flushing.

Garbo looked from her cheeks to his friend's. Steve's face was bright red by the time he made it over to them.

"Happy birthday, asshole," he said, panting.

Garbo looked at him, shocked. "You remembered?"

Steve's cock-eyed grin shifted between Sally and the birthday boy. "Sure thing."

"No one ever remembers..." Garbo said, mystified, his eyes searching the ground.

"It was Sally here that reminded me, you know." Steven winked at her.

Garbo looked up. "What?"

"She's class secretary, Garb. She keeps track of everyone's birthdays and stuff. Posts it on the calendar by the attendance office. Me and Rogie were arm wrestling on the bench right there and saw it. Your name. Happy birthday."

"Thanks," he said. It was all he could muster. He looked back at Sally.

She was smiling at Steve. "I'm glad someone notices all of my hard work."

Steve nodded. "Well, I sure do, Sally-baby." He paused, glancing at his watch. "I gotta split. Still have some calc to finish. Catch ya both later!"

As he turned and sprinted towards the building, Sally reached over and touched Garbo's arm. "Really, though. Happy birthday," she said.

His sheepish smile returned. "Thanks."

She tilted her head. "But I didn't get you a present."

"That's OK. Really. I'm used to people forgetting."

"It's not OK," she said, stomping her foot. Her eyes spanned the parking lot and all of the students milling towards the building. "Come with me," she said finally as she dragged him towards the soccer field behind the school.

He let himself be dragged because it was Sally Stube.

"What are we doing here?" he asked.

"I thought maybe I'd dance with you," she said, a dull shine in her eyes.

He took a step back. "Dance? I don't really, well, I'm not so coordinated."

Her laughter sprayed the air like melted glass fragments. "You'll be surprised, Garbo, how coordinated you become when it's me you're dancing with."

She held out her hand, and he took it. Gently pulling him close to her, she wrapped her arms loosely and comfortably around his back.

"You're so tense," she teased. "Relax. See how easily that tree can sway in the breeze? Make like a tree and dance with me."

He couldn't help but laugh. "Make like a tree. OK."

She laughed at his awkwardness and drew back slightly. "Hmm. Maybe you need some music." She nodded her head in agreement with her assessment. "See if this helps." Drawing him even closer to her, she began to sing, "Happy birthday to you..." Her voice was husky, not at all like he'd imagined, but it was nice nonetheless.

He felt himself relax into her easy sway as she sang the song three times through, humming it the last time. As the first bell rang in the building, she pulled away from him, her smile bright and tenacious.

"Happy birthday, Garbo," she said with a wink.

"Thanks," he said, his voice garbled.

Turning, she half-walked, half-skipped into the building, leaving a melted Garbo on the field.

It was the only time they ever danced together.

Without realizing it, he had stopped walking on the path. As the bittersweet image of Sally walking away from him, her ponytail swaying in rhythm with her stride, sifted out of his thought, he was reminded of why he chose not to think of the past as his body involuntarily doubled over, his hands resting on his knees.

"Mister, are you OK?"

The voice startled him, and he jumped. Slack-jawed, he stared at the mouth that had spoken to him. It belonged to a boy, probably twelve-years-old. Swallowing hard, he felt his head begin to nod. "Yeah, kid, I'm OK. Thanks."

The boy seemed uncertain, but he merely shrugged and continued walking down the path.

Garbo watched his retreat and envied his youth. Sighing, he straightened himself and continued his walk. He wished he hadn't taken the time to remember it was his birthday, to remember Sally or Roger or Steve. There was nothing he could do about it now, though, he told himself.

Cocking his head to the side, he admired the lower branches on the trees, the wooden fingers brushed with satin leaves. Some of the trees still had buds, but most of them had fallen away. Staring at some of the once-beautiful pink petals caking the forest floor, he felt akin to them. Maybe he had been cast to the forest floor just as carelessly, just as naturally. Maybe he'd done the casting himself.

He never minded being alone. Not then, not now.

After graduation, he had gone to college three hours away. Steve and Sally had gone to different universities and Roger had joined the Marines. Garbo never saw much of any of them after the summer of good-bye parties had dwindled to a close. And he was the only one who came back permanently to the valley of their youth. He didn't know where the rest of them were now. It took too much effort to care, though, so he tried not to think about them too much.

He had gone to school to be a photojournalist but graduated with a degree in conservation. After a professor told his first journalism class that they could drop out of school and get a job at a newspaper without any degree or credentials, he decided the program wasn't for him. He wanted to be involved in a program that cared as much about him as he cared about it. Nature had always been his calling.

His professor was right about one thing, though. He didn't need a journalism degree to be hired by the Ridgewood Gazette. He wrote the occasional music review and took pictures for the social pages. Every Earth Day, he exercised his right as a degree-holding Conservationist to preach the gospel of recycling and proper energy use. As much as he loved nature, he loved his camera more and never pushed for more of a scientific role on the paper.

Sally had pushed him into photography. Pausing in his stride, he smiled, remembering that she was the first one who encouraged him to pursue anything. As freshmen on the yearbook staff, they had little clout and less say as to what went in the final edition. One afternoon, though, they were trudging across the soccer field to football practice to take pictures of the players. Sally had the camera, a school-issued rat trap of a machine that was noisy and unreliable. It had been a rainy day, and the field was wet. Garbo didn't mind it. He had on his usual worn-in tennis shoes, but Sally... Sweet old Sally had on her cutest pair of pink foam sandals, at least three inches thick, and complemented by a large plastic daisy on each shoe. Even Garbo, who reserved judgment on everyone and everything, couldn't help but do a double take when he saw Sally Stube trudge through the muck in those shoes.

In October, no less.

With her walking at least half a step ahead of him, Garbo couldn't help but watch her squish in the mud. "Hey, maybe you would rather I did this assignment alone?" he ventured.

She shot him a look. "What would make you even think that, Garbo? I am perf..."

The words lost their importance as her ankle twisted, and she stumbled toward the ground. Her arms jetting out from her body, her eyes wide in surprise, Sally Stube landed in the mud with a sickening splat. Garbo immediately squatted beside her, offering his hand to help her back up. Looking defeated, Sally allowed him to help her.

"Oh god...." she said as she tried desperately to brush off the rash of mud spreading across her pant leg.

With his cheeks flushing brighter than hers, he stood by awkwardly. "Are you... um. Are you OK?"

She glared at him. "Yes." Softening a bit, she extended the camera out to him. "But maybe I'd better let you handle this assignment."

He accepted the slightly muddied contraption and watched her stalk off the field with raw determination. It was at that moment, watching her walk, that he noticed something about the human body that he'd never noticed before. There was something captivating about the blend of arrogance and innocence in Sally's stride. Without thinking about it too much, Garbo lifted the camera and began to photograph her retreat.

*Click.* Blond-haired female headed across hazy mud-streaked field towards gray-brick building dressed in ankle-length blue jeans, pink shirt, and, yes, hideous pink shoes. Facing building. Posture straight and confident. Movement: left leg slightly forward, right leg almost still except for heel slightly turned up, left arm swung out away from body, right arm resting on back of neck, blond hair tucked over left shoulder except for a few stragglers across back.

*Click.* Same female, same setting. Movement: left leg flat, toes pointed to left, right leg also flat, toes pointed more towards building, left arm crooked at the elbow, fingers towards body, right hand on top of head which has turned in profile, hair swung around with movement of head.

*Click.* Same female, same setting. Movement: figure has pivoted body, facing lens instead of building. Left leg flat on ground, right foot tapping toe, left arm on left hip, right arm on right hip. Hair over left shoulder.

"What the hell are you doing, Garbo?" the figure yelled.

Startled, he dropped the camera from his eye. "I... I mean, well... I was..."

"What a pervert! You were taking pictures of my ass for the yearbook! Did you think I wouldn't hear that stupid camera winding to the next shot? I can't believe it, Garb. I thought you were, I dunno, more *normal* than most guys. But you're just as depraved as the rest of them."

He opened his mouth to protest, but he figured his words would be lost on her hot head. Humbled and humiliated, he turned and trudged towards the football field to complete his assignment.

Almost a week went by before she would speak to him again, and then it was only because she forgot that she wasn't supposed to be talking to him. She sat down next to him in biology to ask for help on an algebra problem. Red-faced, he showed her how to do it. She noticed his discomfort as the easy lines on her face tensed, and she drew back.

"How did the pictures come out?" she asked.

He shrugged. "Good."

"The football team or my ass?" she retorted.

He looked at the math problem on his desk and picked his pencil up. Correcting a mistake she'd made on another question, he said, "I wasn't taking pictures of your... I mean, I wasn't trying to... I'm not that sort of... I mean..."

She looked at him skeptically. "Then what were you doing?"

He attempted to look her in the eye. "It was just the way you were, you know, walking. I thought it was interesting."

Cocking her head to the side, she leaned far back in her desk. "The way I walk is interesting."

"Well, it was that day." His cheeks burned mercilessly.

"Let me see the pictures," she said flatly.

"They're in the yearbook office," he said.

"After school, then." With that, she grabbed her homework off his desk and moved back to her own seat.

His palms were sweaty by the time the last bell rang. She cornered him in the hallway after the final class and marched him to the yearbook room. Entering, he opened the door in the filing cabinet with all of the photo proofs and negatives. Extracting the folder labeled "Football," he pulled the pictures out.

"So you were going to leave me in with the football players?" she asked.

He shrugged. "I just left all of the pictures together, that's all."

She grabbed the pictures out of his hand. Hers were on the top of the stack. He watched her face change from indignant cynicism to genuine surprise as she looked at the first picture.

"Garbo..." she sputtered, sitting down. "Garbo, this is really a good picture."

He sat down awkwardly across the table from her. "Thanks."

She flipped to the next photo. And the next. She lined the three of her up next to each other. Looking up at him, she said, "How did you do this?"

He blinked. "Do what?" He leaned over to look at the pictures.

She shook her head slowly. "I'm.... I'm not sure. But somehow, you seem to have captured.... something in these pictures. Even with that horrible excuse for a camera..."

"All I did was watch you walk and push a button..."

She wasn't listening. Instead, she had moved on to the other pictures in the folder, the ones of the football players. She looked at each carefully, meticulously. Garbo sat dumbfounded, unsure of what she saw. Twenty minutes later, she had laid each of the photographs out, story board style, and seemed dazed.

"If Mr. Zim ever sends us on photo assignment again, you are definitely taking the pictures, Garbo. These are incredible." She looked at him with surprised admiration. "Really."

That day, Garbo Proctor decided that he wanted to be a photographer and capture images that would light the fires in Sally's eyes.

Kicking a tiny stone on the path, Garbo smiled bitterly at how different dreams and reality could be. By the time he was a senior, he was yearbook Editor-in-Chief Sally's principle photographer. His byline appeared on almost every page. But as for Sally, all she would do was dance with him on his birthday and flirt with his best friend.

Hands in his pocket, he ambled towards the edge of the forest's shadows. Ahead was Marshall Johnson Field, drenched in sunlight and full of youthful promise. Memories alone could not undo him because he never put more emphasis on any day but today. Whistling again, he emerged from the cave of trees into the blistering light of the afternoon sun.

*About the Author*

An Ohio native, Sarah Wolf moved to Boston in 2002 to earn an MFA in Creative Writing from Emerson College. With a publishing history that spans back to 1994, her most recent publications include the novel *Neverland, Ohio*, the short story collection *Black Ohio Skies*, the poetry volume *There are Phases to These Things*, and the collection of writing *Three Hundred Sixty-five for Two Thousand Eleven*.